'No piece
deserves its

THE IRISH TIMES

Not only is *The Weaver's Grave* one of the best pieces of fiction in Irish literature, it is also one of the best-loved.

This pastoral drama narrates with deceptive simplicity the arguments of two old men over the proper site for the weaver's burial. As their absurd, comic controversy rages, new love and life begin for his youthful widow.

This book contains Seumas O'Kelly's acknowledged masterpiece and a selection of his finest stories. It reveals an extraordinary talent.

SEUMAS O'KELLY

O'Kelly was born in Loughrea, Co. Galway, in 1880. He was friendly with leading literary and political figures at a crucial time in Ireland's history. He wrote plays, novels and verse, but is best remembered now for his stories and his novella, *The Weaver's Grave*. His plays include *The Shuiler's Child, The Bribe, Driftwood* and *Meadowsweet* and were produced by the Abbey Theatre in its early days. His novels are *The Lady of Deerpark* and *Wet Clay* and his stories were collected in *By the Stream of Kilmeen, Waysiders, Hillsiders*, and *The Golden Barque and the Weaver's Grave*.

Seumas O'Kelly was active in Sinn Féin and the Gaelic League and he also edited various newspapers, including *Nationality* when Arthur Griffith was arrested.

THE WEAVER'S GRAVE
is part of the
Classic Irish Fiction Series
edited by Peter Fallon
and published by
The O'Brien Press Dublin

Seumas O'Kelly

THE WEAVER'S GRAVE

Seumas O'Kelly's masterpiece
and a selection of his
short stories

Introduced by Benedict Kiely

The O'Brien Press Dublin

PUBLISHED 1984 BY THE O'BRIEN PRESS LTD.
20 VICTORIA ROAD, DUBLIN 6, IRELAND
FIRST PAPERBACK EDITION 1989

British Cataloguing in Publication Data
O'Kelly, Seumas
The weaver's grave.—(Classic Irish Fiction,
ISSN 0332-1347 :6)
I. Title II. Series
823'.912 [F] PR6029.K4

ISBN 0-86278-152-3 (paperback)

BOOK DESIGN: MICHAEL O'BRIEN
TYPESETTING: REDSETTER LTD.
COVER PAINTING: MARTIN GALE
PRINTING: GUERNSEY PRESS CO. LTD
GUERNSEY, CHANNEL ISLANDS

CONTENTS

The editor and publisher would like
to dedicate this edition
to the memory of Alphonsus Sweeney
in recognition of his help and
with regard to his devoted championship
of his uncle's work.

Introduction

SEUMAS O'KELLY was fascinated by whorls and intricacies and had a superb ability in describing them. When Paul Jennings, the young estate agent of Deerpark, promoted to that dubious office by his father's sudden death, enters the great drawing-room into the presence of Miss Heffernan, the lady of Deerpark, he finds that room as disorderly yet as orderly as some auction mart just before a big sale of antiques. But the antiques were not the remnants of scores of broken homes, of dead romances, of rising and falling fortunes or family flights, but the collection of a family which had bred treasure-seekers from generation to generation:

'That grand medley of personal family property lay stacked along by the walls, piled in the corners, heaped up on shelves, sticking out of overflowing presses: curios and relics, pieces of rare furniture, primitive war-weapons from the East, unknown things of fantastic shape sewn roughly into faded calico covers, great solid iron-bound chests piled one upon the other . . . . Here was the shape of a harp in a shroud, leaning against, as it were, the enormous antlers of an elk. A stuffed Irish wolfhound stood nobly on the upturned bottom of a primitive canoe which had sailed down God only knows what African forest river. Pictures of generations of Heffernans lay stacked in their frames against the walls, a grand procession of splendid gentlemen whose very memories were thus brought into obloquy.'

That great room is every bit as much a house of the dead

as the graveyard of Cloon na Morav, that ultimate accumulation of the past. In that same novel to which the lady of Deerpark gives its title, Paul Jennings listens to the lady playing on that harp polkas and minuets:

'So powerfully did I feel the effects of the music that it seemed to me all the Heffernans, men and women, stepped down from their pictures on the walls and danced about the room. There they were, stout gentlemen in their powdered wigs, their green or red silk coats, white silk knee-breeches, shoes with silver buckles, going round and round in the lilting polka, making little springs now and again as if the spirit of levity was moving their staid souls, all attention to the tall dames in the bright dresses, their long earrings shaking about their ears, beauty spots on their cheeks, diamonds flashing on their necks, fans half-hiding their coquetting faces. A young pair dashed down the full length of the room, unconscious and uncaring for the couples they elbowed out of their steps, and as they came along they showed their white teeth, their brilliant eyes, their bodies swinging together, kicking their heels in sheer delight, a pair of lovers taking life at the noontide.

'A group of onlookers stood at the end of the room, critical spectators of the dance, helping themselves now and again to pinches of snuff from silver boxes, dusting the snuff from their ruffles with lace handkerchiefs which they carried in their sleeves. The polka stopped suddenly, but was followed by a minuet, when another set of dancers, more stately than the last, took the floor, several old bucks putting out their legs, encased in silk hose, with (a) pride . . .'

The dance goes on. For a brief moment in a tragic story the harp is out of its shroud and liberated from the antlers of the ancient elk. There is such humour and fantasy in the passage that it is a shock to realise that we have been amused and stimulated by the antics of ghosts, that we have been watching a dance of death, that Seumas O'Kelly may have been, as T. S. Eliot said Webster was, much possessed by death. His masterpiece, *The Weaver's Grave,* with all its dark humour was, indeed, inspired by graves and old bones and the spectacle of contorted age.

The Lady of Deerpark was published in 1917 when O'Kelly was in his mid-thirties. It is as awkward in many ways as Thomas Hardy's strange early novel, *Desperate Remedies*. It is also, and in many passages, as valuably revealing. 'What a child of life I was', the narrator, Jennings, says in the middle of a quite impossible episode which, for want of anything else to call it, we may call a love-episode. The novelist could well have been speaking for himself.

Up to the appearance of that sad, doomed lady, Miss Heffernan, O'Kelly's creative work had been almost entirely in the theatre, the exception being his first publication, which he described as a sketch and stories, *By the Stream of Kilmeen* (1906). Five plays in all up to *The Bribe*, published in 1914, which, in the company of the late Gabriel Fallon, I saw impressively revived in the 1940s. But in *The Lady of Deerpark*, he displayed, spasmodically it is true, most impressive powers.

His life was short and uneventful up to the tragic event that aggravated his unstable health condition and, in 1918, caused his premature death, and brought him, in the mood and fashion of the time, the sad glory of being a patriot martyr. His funeral was, (and I have spoken to people who were there), even for Irish patriot funerals of the time, most moving. His reputation, personal and literary, was a sort of quiet legend not known to many but deeply cherished by the few: until Micheál Ó hAodha's adaptation of *The Weaver's Grave* won the *Prix D'Italia* and brought a work of genius to the notice of many. This reprint should complete the work of revival.

Padraic Fallon, in a splendid poem which he modestly said was after the Irish of Raftery, wrote of Loughrea as 'that old dead city where the weavers / Have pined at the mouldering looms since Helen broke the thread . . .', which old dead city was, aptly enough, the birthplace of Seumas O'Kelly in 1878 or 1880, there is some doubt about the date.

His father was a prosperous corn-factor and, in his early twenties, the son, who had gone into provincial journalism, became editor of *The Southern Star* in Skibbereen, the youngest editor, it was said, in Ireland. Very early on he joined Arthur Griffith's Sinn Féin movement. In 1906 he moved to Naas as editor of *The Leinster Leader*. Then from 1912-1915 he edited in Dublin the *Saturday Evening Post*. But ill-health forced him to retire for, earlier on, he had had an attack of rheumatic fever which affected his heart. Later on he shared a house in Dublin with the poet Seamus O'Sullivan who, many years afterwards, I heard speak of him with warm affection in the company of Austin Clarke, M. J. MacManus, R. M. Smyllie and Cathal O'Shannon. Seamus O'Sullivan was not notorious for speaking with affection to or about many.

When Arthur Griffith was arrested, O'Kelly stood in for him as editor of the paper *Nationality*. I quote here from Anne Clune who has written in *The Irish Short Story* (eds. Rafroidi and Brown) one of the two most useful studies of O'Kelly:

'Three days after the armistice, soldiers and their wives, incensed by Sinn Féin policies on the war, invaded and wrecked the offices of *Nationality*. After they had left O'Kelly was found unconscious, (some accounts say that he tried to defend himself and the printing presses with his walking stick), and did not recover consciousness. . . . . Sinn Féin, in recognition of O'Kelly's complete lack of self-interest in carrying on Griffith's work, and in view of the events preceding his collapse, gave him a hero's funeral.'

The other study of O'Kelly is by Aidan O'Hanlon and is to be found in *The Capuchin Annual* of 1949. From it I quote a fragment of what Seamus O'Sullivan wrote down about his friend: 'His was, indeed, one of those rare natures which have the faculty of spreading a sense of well-being, of security, good fellowship, healing, by their very presence. Bitterness seemed to fade out in the presence of Seumas O'Kelly, and quarrelling was impossible when he was in the company . . . . yet beneath that gentleness lay hidden a very real strength which could evince itself splendidly when occasion demanded . . . .'

O'Kelly worked in the novel, the short-story, the theatre, and there is also a book of passable and interesting verse. For a short life crowded with idealistic politics and with the day-to-day drag of journalism, and spancelled by ill-health, the literary production was considerable. His novel, *Wet Clay*, takes its place with Shan F. Bullock's *Dan the Dollar* as a serious effort to consider the social implications of what used to be called the Returned American. In his play *The Country Dressmaker* George Fitzmaurice had made the most of the comic possibilities of the type at the time, and George Moore had dealt with the matter in a melancholy way in *The Untilled Field*.

But in the case of O'Kelly it is when we put a foot on the stile that gives us access to Cloon na Morav that we right-away recognise greatness: 'Mortimer Hehir, the weaver, had died, and they had come in search of his grave to Cloon na Morav, the Meadow of the Dead . . .'

Thirty-four years ago, writing about O'Kelly, I had something like this to say: That story of old men is as rigid as the stony places of Galway: it is all nails and stones and the pull of the earth on the bodies of men. It is more conscious of the earth than anything in Irish literature since William Carleton's people appeared like the animals in Milton's Paradise, 'half-emerged only from the earth and its brooding', to quote for the ninetieth time the young Mr. Yeats. It is grotesque and hard and stiff and twisted, a tale of old men and graves, and the agreements and disagreements of old men, a study of sparse soil in perpetual struggle with rocks, of rocks standing out endlessly against the assault of the ocean. The story is like a twisted hawthorn bush bent from the sea by the beating of the wind, sinewy roots holding to thin soil in the shelter of a grey stone wall.

The young widow of the ancient weaver, indeed, thinks

of old men and trees in a way that reminds me of Webster's Bosola, (Webster again!) comparing two mighty noblemen to plum-trees that grow crooked over standing pools. The likeness of old men to old trees occurs to her in 'their crankiness, their complexity, their angles, their very barks, bulges, gnarled twistiness and kinks', and it 'brought a sense of oppression to the sorely-tried brain of the widow'.

That, more-or-less as I wrote it, was thirty-four years ago and it occurs to me now that the land around the old dead city of the weavers is not all that inhospitable, and that I may have been too harsh on the old men. They may be neither amiable nor attractive nor have the glow of sunset clouds about them. But they are imperishably alive and the Meadow of the Dead is as immortal as the Fenian meadows where Goll wrestled with God. The mounds hide the loved and honoured dead, but the Meadow is a living reservoir of memory and tradition, and the most gnarled old tree has strong, undying roots. Look at that last great passage that centres around the vision and satisfaction of the widow and her discovery of youth and of love:

'The widow thought that the world was strange, the sky extraordinary, the man's head against the red sky a wonder, a poem, above it the sparkle of the great young star.'

Benedict Kiely

Part One

The Weaver's Grave

I

MORTIMER HEHIR, the weaver, had died and they had come in search of his grave to Cloon na Morav, the Meadow of the Dead. Meehaul Lynskey, the nail-maker, was first across the stile. There was excitement in his face. His long warped body moved in a shuffle over the ground. Following him came Cahir Bowes, the stone-breaker, who was so beaten down from the hips forward, that his back was horizontal as the back of an animal. His right hand held a stick which propped him up in front, his left hand clutched his coat behind, just above the small of the back. By these devices he kept himself from toppling head over heels as he walked. Mother earth was the brow of Cahir Bowes by magnetic force, and Cahir Bowes was resisting her fatal kiss to the last. And just now there was animation in the face he raised from its customary contemplation of the ground. Both old men had the air of those who had been unexpectedly let loose. For a long time they had lurked somewhere in the shadows of life, the world having no business for them, and now, suddenly, they had been remembered and called forth to perform an office which nobody else on earth could perform. The excitement in their faces as they crossed over the stile into Cloon na Morav expressed a vehemence in their belated usefulness. Hot on their heels came two dark, handsome, stoutly built men, alike even to the cord that tied their corduroy trousers under their knees, and, being grave-diggers, they carried flashing spades. Last of all, and after a little delay, a firm white hand was laid on the stile, a dark figure followed, the figure of a woman whose palely sad face was picturesquely, almost dramatically, framed in a black shawl which hung from the crown of the head. She was the widow of Mortimer Hehir, the weaver, and she followed the others into Cloon na Morav, the Meadow of the Dead.

To glance at Cloon na Morav as you went by on the hilly road, was to get an impression of a very old burial-ground; to pause on the road and look at Cloon na Morav was to become conscious of its quiet situation, of winds singing down from the hills in a chant for the dead; to walk over to the wall and look at the mounds inside was to provoke quotations from Gray's 'Elegy'; to make the sign of the Cross, lean over the wall, observe the gloomy lichened background of the wall opposite, and mark the things that seemed to stray about, like yellow snakes in the grass, was to think of Hamlet moralizing at the graveside of Ophelia, and hear him establish the identity of Yorick. To get over the stile and stumble about inside, was to forget all these things and to know Cloon na Morav for itself. Who could tell the age of Cloon na Morav? The mind could only swoon away into mythology, paddle about in the dotage of paganism, the toothless infancy of Christianity. How many generations, how many septs, how many clans, how many families, how many people, had gone into Cloon na Morav? The mind could only take wing on the romances of mathematics. The ground was billowy, grotesque. Several partially suppressed insurrections — a great thirsting, worming, pushing and shouldering under the sod — had given it character. A long tough growth of grass wired it from end to end. Nature, by this effort, endeavouring to control the strivings of the more daring of the insurgents of Cloon na Morav. No path here; no plan or map or register existed; if there ever had been one or the other it had been lost. Invasions and wars and famines and feuds had swept the ground and left it. All claims to interment had been based on powerful traditional rights. These rights had years ago come to an end — all save in a few outstanding cases, the rounding up of a spent generation.

The overflow from Cloon na Morav had already set a new cemetery on its legs a mile away, a cemetery in which limestone headstones and Celtic crosses were springing up like mushrooms, advertising the triviality of a civilization of men and women, who, according to their own epitaphs, had done exactly the two things they could not very well avoid doing: they had all, their obituary notices said, been born and they had all died. Obscure quotations from Scripture were sometimes added by way of apology. There was an almost unanimous expression of forgiveness to the Lord for what had happened to the deceased. None of this lack of humour in Cloon na Morav. Its monuments were comparatively few, and such of them as it had not swallowed were well within the general atmosphere. No obituary notice in the place was complete; all were either wholly or partially eaten up by the teeth of time. The monuments that had made a stout battle for existence were pathetic in their futility. The vanity of the fashionable of dim ages made one weep. Who on earth could have brought in the white marble slab to Cloon na Morav? It had grown green with shame. Perhaps the lettering, once readable upon it, had been conscientiously picked out in gold. The shrieking winds and the fierce rains of the hills alone could tell. Plain heavy stones, their shoulders rounded with a chisel, presumably to give them some off-handed resemblance to humanity, now swooned at fantastic angles from their settings, as if the people to whose memory they had been dedicated had shouldered them away as an impertinence. Other slabs lay in fragments on the ground, filling the mind with thoughts of Moses descending from Mount Sinai and, waxing angry at sight of his followers dancing about false gods, casting the stone tables containing the Commandments to the ground, breaking them in pieces — the most tragic destruction of a first edition that the world has known. Still other heavy square dark slabs, surely creatures of a pagan imagination, were laid flat down on numerous short legs, looking sometimes like representations of monstrous black cockroaches, and again like tables at which the guests of Cloon na Morav might sit down, goblin-like, in the moonlight, when nobody was looking. Most of the legs had given way and the tables lay overturned, as if there had been a quarrel at cards the night before. Those that had kept their legs exhibited great cracks or fissures across their backs, like slabs of dark ice breaking up. Over by the wall, draped in its pattern of dark green lichen, certain families of dim ages had made an effort to keep up the traditions of the Eastern sepulchres. They had showed an aristocratic reluctance to take to the common clay in Cloon na Morav. They had built low casket-shaped houses against the gloomy wall, putting an enormously heavy iron door with ponderous iron rings — like the rings on a pier by the sea — at one end, a tremendous lock — one wondered what Goliath kept the key — finally cementing the whole thing up and surrounding it with spiked iron railings. In these contraptions very aristocratic families locked up their dead as if they were dangerous wild animals. But these ancient vanities only heightened the general democracy of the ground. To prove a traditional right to a place in its community was to have the bond of your pedigree sealed. The act of burial in Cloon na Morav was in itself an epitaph. And it was amazing to think that there were two people still over the sod who had such a right — one Mortimer Hehir, the weaver, just passed away, the other Malachi Roohan, a cooper, still breathing. When these two survivors of a great generation got tucked under the sward of Cloon na Morav its terrific history would, for all practical purposes, have ended.

II

Meehaul Lynskey, the nailer, hitched forward his bony shoulders and cast his eyes over the ground — eyes that were small and sharp, but unaccustomed to range over wide spaces. The width and the wealth of Cloon na Morav were baffling to him. He had spent his long life on the look-out for one small object so that he might hit it. The colour that he loved was the golden glowing end of a stick of burning iron; wherever he saw that he seized it in a small sconce at the end of a long handle, wrenched it off by a twitch of the wrist, hit it with a flat hammer several deft taps, dropped it into a vessel of water, out of which it came a cool and perfect nail. To do this thing several hundred times six days in the week, and pull the chain of a bellows at short intervals, Meehaul Lynskey had developed an extraordinary dexterity of sight and touch, a swiftness of business that no mortal man could exceed, and so long as he had been pitted against nail-makers of flesh and blood he had more than held his own; he had, indeed, even put up a tremendous but an unequal struggle against the competition of nail-making machinery. Accustomed as he was to concentrate on a single, glowing, definite object, the complexity and disorder of Cloon na Morav unnerved him. But he was not going to betray any of these professional defects to Cahir Bowes, the stone-breaker. He had been sent there as an ambassador by the caretaker of Cloon na Morav, picked out for his great age, his local knowledge, and his good character, and it was his business to point out to the twin grave-diggers, sons of the caretaker, the weaver's grave, so that it might be opened to receive him. Meehaul Lynskey had a knowledge of the place, and was quite certain as to a great number of grave sites, while the caretaker, being an official without records, had a profound ignorance of the whole place.

Cahir Bowes followed the drifting figure of the nail-maker over the ground, his face hitched up between his shoulders, his eyes keen and grey, glint-like as the mountains of stones he had in his day broken up as road material. Cahir, no less than Meehaul, had his knowledge of Cloon na Morav and some of his own people were buried here. His sharp, clear eyes took in the various mounds with the eye of a prospector. He, too, had been sent there as an ambassador, and as between himself and Meehaul Lynskey he did not think that there could be any two opinions; his knowledge was superior to the knowledge of the nailer. Whenever Cahir Bowes met a loose stone on the grass, quite instinctively he turned it over with his stick, his sharp old eyes judging its grain with a professional swiftness, then cracking at it with his stick. If the stick were a hammer the stone, attacked on its most vulnerable spot, would fall to pieces like glass. In stones Cahir Bowes saw not sermons but seams. Even the headstones he tapped significantly with the ferrule of his stick, for Cahir Bowes had an artist's passion for his art, though his art was far from creative. He was one of the great destroyers, the reducers, the makers of chaos, a powerful and remorseless critic of the Stone Age.

The two old men wandered about Cloon na Morav, in no hurry whatever to get through with their business. After all they had been a long time pensioned off, forgotten, neglected by the world. The renewed sensation of usefulness was precious to them. They knew that when this business was over they were not likely to be in request for anything in this world again. They were ready to oblige the world, but the world would have to allow them their own time. The world, made up of the two grave-diggers and the widow of the weaver, gathered all this without any vocal proclamation. Slowly, mechanically as it were, they followed the two ancients about Cloon na Morav. And the two ancients wandered about with the labour of age and the hearts of children. They separated, wandered about silently as if they were picking up old acquaintances, stumbling upon forgotten things, gathering up the threads of days that were over, reviving their memories, and then drew together, beginning to talk slowly, almost casually, and all their talk was of the dead, of the people who lay in the ground about them. They warmed to it, airing their knowledge, calling up names and complications of family relationships, telling stories, reviving all virtues, whispering at past vices, past vices that did not sound like vices at all, for the long years are great mitigators and run in splendid harness with the coyest of all the virtues, Charity. The whispered scandals of Cloon na

Morav were seen by the twin grave-diggers and the widow of the weaver through such a haze of antiquity that they were no longer scandals but romances. The rake and the drab, seen a good way down the avenue, merely look picturesque. The grave-diggers rested their spades in the ground, leaning on the handles in exactly the same graveyard pose, and the pale widow stood in the background, silent, apart, patient, and, like all dark, tragic-looking women, a little mysterious.

The stone-breaker pointed with his quivering stick at the graves of the people whom he spoke about. Every time he raised that forward support one instinctively looked, anxious and fearful, to see if the clutch were secure on the small of the back. Cahir Bowes had the sort of shape that made one eternally fearful for his equilibrium. The nailer, who, like his friend the stone-breaker, wheezed a good deal, made short, sharp gestures, and always with the right hand; the fingers were hooked in such a way, and he shot out the arm in such a manner, that they gave the illusion that he held a hammer and that it was struck out over a very hot fire. Every time Meehaul Lynskey made this gesture one expected to see sparks flying.

'Where are we to bury the weaver?' one of the grave-diggers asked at last.

Both old men laboured around to see where the interruption, the impertinence had come from. They looked from one twin to the other, with gravity, indeed anxiety, for they were not sure which was which, or if there was not some illusion in the resemblance, some trick of youth to baffle age.

'Where are we to bury the weaver?' the other twin repeated, and the strained look on the old men's faces deepened. They were trying to fix in their minds which of the twins had interrupted first and which last. The eyes of Meehaul Lynskey fixed on one twin with the instinct of his trade, while Cahir Bowes ranged both and eventually wandered to the figure of the widow in the background, silently accusing her of impatience in a matter in which it would be indelicate for her to show haste.

'We can't stay here for ever,' said the first twin.

It was the twin upon whom Meehaul Lynskey had fastened his small eyes, and, sure of his man this time, Meehaul Lynskey hit him.

'There's many a better man than you,' said Meehaul Lynskey, 'that will stay here for ever.' He swept Cloon na Morav with the hooked fingers.

'Them that stays in Cloon na Morav for ever,' said Cahir Bowes with a wheezing energy, 'have nothing to be ashamed of — nothing to be ashamed of. Remember that, young fellow.'

Meehaul Lynskey did not seem to like the intervention, the help, of Cahir Bowes. It was a sort of implication that he had not — *he*, mind you, — had not hit the nail properly on the head.

'Well, where are we to bury him, anyway?' said the twin, hoping to profit by the chagrin of the nailer — the nailer who, by implication, had failed to nail.

'You'll bury him,' said Meehaul Lynskey, 'where all belonging to him is buried.'

'We come,' said the other twin, 'with some sort of intention of that kind.' He drawled out the words, in imitation of the old men. The skin relaxed on his handsome dark face and then bunched in puckers of humour about the eyes; Meehaul Lynskey's gaze, wandering for once, went to the handsome dark face of the other twin and the skin relaxed and then bunched in puckers of humour about *his* eyes, so that Meehaul Lynskey had an unnerving sensation that these young grave-diggers were purposely confusing him.

'You'll bury him,' he began with some vehemence, and was amazed to again find Cahir Bowes taking the words out of his mouth, snatching the hammer out of his hand, so to speak.

'—— where you're told to bury him,' Cahir Bowes finished for him.

Meehaul Lynskey was so hurt that his long slanting figure moved away down the graveyard, then stopped suddenly. He had determined to do a dreadful thing. He had determined to do a thing that was worse than kicking a crutch from under a cripple's shoulder; that was like stealing the holy water out of a room where a man lay dying. He had determined to ruin the last day's amusement on this earth for Cahir Bowes and himself by prematurely and basely disclosing the weaver's grave!

'Here,' called back Meehaul Lynskey, 'is the weaver's grave, and here you will bury him.'

All moved down to the spot, Cahir Bowes going with extraordinary spirit, the ferrule of his terrible stick cracking on the stones he met on the way.

'Between these two mounds,' said Meehaul Lynskey, and already the twins raised their twin spades in a sinister movement, like swords of lancers flashing at a drill.

'Between these two mounds,' said Meehaul Lynskey 'is the grave of Mortimer Hehir.'

'Hold on!' cried Cahir Bowes. He was so eager, so excited, that he struck one of the grave-diggers a whack of his stick on the back. Both grave-diggers swung about to him as if both had been hurt by the one blow.

'Easy there,' said the first twin.

'Easy there,' said the second twin.

'Easy yourselves,' cried Cahir Bowes. He wheeled about his now quivering face on Meehaul Lynskey.

'What is it you're saying about the spot between the mounds?' he demanded.

'I'm saying,' said Meehaul Lynskey vehemently, 'that it's the weaver's grave.'

'What weaver?' asked Cahir Bowes.

'Mortimer Hehir,' replied Meehaul Lynskey. 'There's no other weaver in it.'

'Was Julia Rafferty a weaver?'

'What Julia Rafferty?'

'The midwife, God rest her.'

'How could she be a weaver if she was a midwife?'

'Not a one of me knows. But I'll tell you what I do know and know rightly: that it's Julia Rafferty is in that place and no weaver at all.'

'Amn't I telling you it's the weaver's grave?'

'And amn't I telling you it's not?'

'That I may be as dead as my father but the weaver was buried there.'

'A bone of a weaver was never sunk in it as long as weavers was weavers. Full of Raffertys it is.'

'Alive with weavers it is.'

'Heavenlyful Father, was the like ever heard: to say that a grave was alive with dead weavers.'

'It's full of them — full as a tick.'

'And the clean grave that Mortimer Hehir was never done boasting about — dry and sweet and deep and no way bulging at all. Did you see the burial of his father ever?'

'I did, in troth, see the burial of his father — forty year ago if it's a day.'

'Forty year ago — it's fifty-one year come the sixteenth of May. It's well I remember it and it's well I have occasion to remember it, for it was the day after that again that myself ran away to join the soldiers, my aunt hot foot after me, she to be buying me out the week after, I a high-spirited fellow morebetoken.'

'Leave the soldiers out of it and leave your aunt out of it and stick to the weaver's grave. Here in this place was the last weaver buried, and I'll tell you what's more. In a straight line with it is the grave of ——'

'A straight line, indeed! Who but yourself, Meehaul Lynskey, ever heard of a straight line in Cloon na Morav? No such thing was ever wanted or ever allowed in it.'

'In a straight direct line, measured with a rule ——'

'Measured with crooked, stumbling feet, maybe feet half reeling in drink.'

'Can't you listen to me now?'

'I was always a bad warrant to listen to anything except

sense. Yourself ought to be the last man in the world to talk about straight lines, you with the sight scattered in your head, with the divil of sparks flying under your eyes.'

'Don't mind me sparks now, nor me sight neither, for in a straight measured line with the weaver's grave was the grave of the Cassidys.'

'What Cassidys?'

'The Cassidys that herded for the O'Sheas.'

'Which O'Sheas?'

'O'Shea Ruadh of Cappakelly. Don't you know anyone at all, or is it gone entirely your memory is?'

'Cappakelly *inagh!* And who cares a whistle about O'Shea Ruadh, he or his seed, breed and generations? It's a rotten lot of landgrabbers they were.'

'Me hand to you on that. Striving ever they were to put their red paws on this bit of grass and that perch of meadow.'

'Hungry in themselves even for the cutaway bog.'

'And Mortimer Hehir a decent weaver, respecting every man's wool.'

'His forehead pallid with honesty over the yard and the loom.'

'If a bit broad-spoken when he came to the door for a smoke of the pipe.'

'Well, there won't be a mouthful of clay between himself and O'Shea Ruadh now.'

'In the end what did O'Shea Ruadh get after all his striving?'

'I'll tell you that. He got what land suits a blind fiddler.'

'Enough to pad the crown of the head and tap the sole of the foot! Now you're talking.'

'And the devil a word out of him now no more than anyone else in Cloon na Morav.'

'It's easy talking to us all about land when we're packed up in our timber boxes.'

'As the weaver was when he got sprinkled with the holy water in that place.'

'As Julia Rafferty was when they read the prayers over her

in that place, she a fine, buxom, cheerful woman in her day, with great skill in her business.'

'Skill or no skill, I'm telling you she's not there, wherever she is.'

'I suppose you want me to take her up in my arms and show her to you?'

'Well then, indeed, Cahir, I do not. 'Tisn't a very handsome pair you would make at all, you not able to stand much more hardship than Julia herself.'

From this there developed a slow, laboured, aged dispute between the two authorities. They moved from grave to grave, pitting memory against memory, story against story, knocking down reminiscence with reminiscence, arguing in a powerful intimate obscurity that no outsider could hope to follow, blasting knowledge with knowledge, until the whole place seemed strewn with the corpses of their arguments. The two grave-diggers followed them about in a grim silence; impatience in their movements, their glances; the widow keeping track of the grand tour with a miserable feeling, a feeling, as site after site was rejected, that the tremendous exclusiveness of Cloon na Morav would altogether push her dead man, the weaver, out of his privilege. The dispute ended, like all epics, where it began. Nothing was established, nothing settled. But the two old men were quite exhausted, Meehaul Lynskey sitting down on the back of one of the monstrous cockroaches, Cahir Bowes leaning against a tombstone that was half-submerged, its end up like the stern of a derelict at sea. Here they sat glaring at each other like a pair of grim vultures.

The two grave-diggers grew restive. Their business had to be done. The weaver would have to be buried. Time pressed. They held a consultation apart. It broke up after a brief exchange of views, a little laughter.

'Meehaul Lynskey is right,' said one of the twins.

Meehaul Lynskey's face lit up. Cahir Bowes looked as if he had been slapped on the cheeks. He moved out from his tombstone.

'Meehaul Lynskey is right,' repeated the other twin. They had decided to break up the dispute by taking sides. They raised their spades and moved to the site which Meehaul had urged upon them.

'Don't touch that place,' Cahir Bowes cried, raising his stick. He was measuring the back of the grave-digger again when the man spun round upon him, menace in his handsome dark face.

'Touch me with that stick,' he cried, 'and I'll ——'

Some movement in the background, some agitation in the widow's shawl, caused the grave-digger's menace to dissolve, the words to die in his mouth, a swift flush mounting the man's face like a flash. It was as if she had cried out, 'Ah, don't touch the poor old, cranky fellow! You might hurt him.' And it was as if the grave-digger had cried back: 'He has annoyed me greatly, but I don't intend to hurt him. And since you say so with your eyes I won't even threaten him.'

Under pressure of the half threat, Cahir Bowes shuffled back a little way, striking an attitude of feeble dignity, leaning out on his stick while the grave-diggers got to work.

'It's the weaver's grave, surely,' said Meehaul Lynskey.

'If it is,' said Cahir Bowes, 'remember his father was buried down seven feet. You gave into that this morning.'

'There was no giving in about it,' said Meehaul Lynskey. 'We all know that one of the wonders of Cloon na Morav was the burial of the last weaver seven feet, he having left it as an injunction on his family. The world knows he went down the seven feet.'

'And remember this,' said Cahir Bowes, 'that Julia Rafferty was buried no seven feet. If she is down three feet it's as much as she went.'

Sure enough, the grave-diggers had not dug down more than three feet of ground when one of the spades struck hollowly on unhealthy timber. The sound was unmistakable and ominous. There was silence for a moment. Then Cahir Bowes made a sudden short spurt up a mound beside him, as if he were some sort of mechanical animal wound up, his horizontal back quivering. On the mound he made a superhuman effort to straighten himself. He got his ears and his blunt nose into a considerable elevation. He had not been so upright for twenty years. And raising his weird countenance, he broke into a cackle that was certainly meant to be a crow. He glared at Meehaul Lynskey, his emotion so great that his eyes swam in a watery triumph.

Meehaul Lynskey had his eyes, as was his custom, upon one thing, and that thing was the grave, and especially the spot on the grave where the spade had struck the coffin. He looked stunned and fearful. His eyes slowly withdrew their gimlet-like scrutiny from the spot, and sought the triumphant crowing figure of Cahir Bowes on the mound.

Meehaul Lynskey looked as if he would like to say something, but no words came. Instead he ambled away, retired from the battle, and standing apart, rubbed one leg against the other, above the back of the ankles, like some great insect. His hooked fingers at the same time stroked the bridge of his nose. He was beaten.

'I suppose it's not the weaver's grave,' said one of the grave-diggers. Both of them looked at Cahir Bowes.

'Well, you know it's not,' said the stone-breaker. 'It's Julia Rafferty you struck. She helped many a one into the world in her day, and it's poor recompense to her to say she can't be at rest when she left it.' He turned to the remote figure of Meehaul Lynskey and cried: 'Ah-ha, well you may rub your ignorant legs. And I'm hoping Julia will forgive you this day's ugly work.'

In silence, quickly, with reverence, the twins scooped back the clay over the spot. The widow looked on with the same quiet, patient, mysterious silence. One of the grave-diggers turned on Cahir Bowes.

'I suppose you know where the weaver's grave is?' he asked.

Cahir Bowes looked at him with an ancient tartness, then said:

'You suppose!'

'Of course, you know where it is.'

Cahir Bowes looked as if he knew where the gates of heaven were and that he might — or might not — enlighten an ignorant world. It all depended! His eyes wandered knowingly out over the meadows beyond the graveyard. He said:

'I do know where the weaver's grave is.'

'We'll be very much obliged to you if you show it to us.'

'Very much obliged,' endorsed the other twin.

The stone-breaker, thus flattered, led the way to a new site, one nearer to the wall, where were the plagiarisms of the Eastern sepulchres. Cahir Bowes made little journeys about, measuring so many steps from one place to another, mumbling strange and unintelligible information to himself, going through an extraordinary geometrical emotion, striking the ground hard taps with his stick.

'Glory be to the Lord,' cried Meehaul Lynskey, 'he's like the man they had driving the water for the well in the quarry field, he whacking the ground with his magic hazel wand.'

Cahir Bowes made no reply. He was too absorbed in his own emotion. A little steam was beginning to ascend from his brow. He was moving about the ground like some grotesque spider weaving an invisible web.

'I suppose now,' said Meehaul Lynskey, addressing the marble monument, 'that as soon as Cahir hits the right spot one of the weavers will turn about below. Or maybe he expects one of them to whistle up at him out of the ground. That's it; devil a other! When we hear the whistle we'll all know for certain where to bury the weaver.'

Cahir Bowes was contracting his movements, so that he was now circling about the one spot, like a dog going to lie down.

Meehaul Lynskey drew a little closer, watching eagerly, his grim yellow face, seared with yellow marks from the fires of his workshop, tightened up in a sceptical pucker. His half-muttered words were bitter with an aged sarcasm. He cried:

'Say nothing; he'll get it yet, will the man of knowledge, the know-all, Cahir Bowes! Give him time. Give him until this day twelve month. Look at that for a right-about-turn on the left heel. Isn't the nimbleness of that young fellow a treat to see? Are they whistling to you from below, Cahir? Is it dancing to the weaver's music you are? That's it, devil a other.'

Cahir Bowes was mapping out a space on the grass with his stick. Gradually it took, more or less, the outline of a grave site. He took off his hat and mopped his steaming brow with a red handkerchief, saying:

'There's the weaver's grave.'

'God in Heaven,' cried Meehaul Lynskey, 'will you look at what he calls the weaver's grave? I'll say nothing at all. I'll hold my tongue. I'll shut up. Not one word will I say about Alick Finlay, the mildest man that ever lived, a man full of religion, never at the end of his prayers! But, sure, it's the saints of God that get the worst of it in this world, and if Alick escaped during life, faith he's in for it now, with the pirates and the bodysnatchers of Cloon na Morav on top of him.'

A corncrake began to sing in the nearby meadow, and his rasping notes sounded like a queer accompaniment to the words of Meehaul Lynskey. The grave-diggers, who had gone to work on the Cahir Bowes site, laughed a little, one of them looking for a moment at Meehaul Lynskey, saying:

'Listen to that damned old corncrake in the meadow! I'd like to put a sod in its mouth.'

The man's eye went to the widow. She showed no emotion one way or the other, and the grave-digger got back to his work. Meehaul Lynskey, however, wore the cap. He said:

'To be sure! I'm to sing dumb. I'm not to have a word out of me at all. Others can rattle away as they like in this place, as if they owned it. The ancient good old stock is to be nowhere and the scruff of the hills let rampage as they will.

That's it, devil a other. Castles falling and dunghills rising! Well, God be with the good old times and the good old mannerly people that used to be in it, and God be with Alick Finlay, the holiest ——'

A sod of earth came through the air from the direction of the grave, and, skimming Meehaul Lynskey's head, dropped somewhere behind. The corncrake stopped his notes in the meadow, and Meehaul Lynskey stood statuesque in a mute protest, and silence reigned in the place while the clay sang up in a swinging rhythm from the grave.

Cahir Bowes, watching the operations with intensity, said:

'It was nearly going astray on me.'

Meehaul Lynskey gave a little snort. He asked:

'What was?'

'The weaver's grave.'

'Remember this: the last weaver is down seven feet. And remember this: Alick Finlay is down less than Julia Rafferty.'

He had no sooner spoken when a fearful thing happened. Suddenly out of the soft cutting of the earth a spade sounded harsh on tinware, there was a crash, less harsh, but painfully distinct, as if rotten boards were falling together, then a distinct subsidence of the earth. The work stopped at once. A moment's fearful silence followed. It was broken by a short, dry laugh from Meehaul Lynskey. He said:

'God be merciful to us all! That's the latter-end of Alick Finlay.'

The two grave-diggers looked at each other. The shawl of the widow in the background was agitated. One twin said to the other:

'This can't be the weaver's grave.'

The other agreed. They all turned their eyes upon Cahir Bowes. He was hanging forward in a pained strain, his head quaking, his fingers twitching on his stick. Meehaul Lynskey turned to the marble monument and said with venom:

'If I was guilty I'd go down on my knees and beg God's pardon. If I didn't I'd know the ghost of Alick Finlay, saint as he was, would leap upon me and guzzle me — for what right would I have to set anybody at him with driving spades when he was long years in his grave?'

Cahir Bowes took no notice. He was looking at the ground, searching about, and slowly, painfully, began his web-spinning again. The grave-diggers covered in the ground without a word. Cahir Bowes appeared to get lost in some fearful maze of his own making. A little whimper broke from him now and again. The steam from his brow thickened in the air, and eventually he settled down on the end of a headstone, having got the worst of it. Meehaul Lynskey sat on another stone facing him, and they glared, sinister and grotesque, at each other.

'Cahir Bowes,' said Meehaul Lynskey, 'I'll tell you what you are, and then you can tell me what I am.'

'Have it whatever way you like,' said Cahir Bowes. 'What is it that I am?'

'You're a gentleman, a grand oul' stone-breaking gentleman. That's what you are, devil a other!'

The wrinkles on the withered face of Cahir Bowes contracted, his eyes stared across at Meehaul Lynskey, and two yellow teeth showed between his lips. He wheezed:

'And do you know what you are?'

'I don't.'

'You're a nailer, that's what you are, a damned nailer.'

They glared at each other in a quaking, grim silence.

And it was at this moment of collapse, of deadlock, that the widow spoke for the first time. At the first sound of her voice one of the twins perked his head, his eyes going to her face. She said in a tone as quiet as her whole behaviour:

'Maybe I ought to go up to the Tunnel Road and ask Malachi Roohan where the grave is.'

They had all forgotten the oldest man of them all, Malachi Roohan. He would be the last mortal man to enter Cloon na Morav. He had been the great friend of Mortimer Hehir, the weaver, in the days that were over, and the whole world knew that. Mortimer Hehir's knowledge of Cloon na Morav was perfect. Maybe Malachi Roohan would have learned a great deal from him. And Malachi Roohan, the cooper, was so long bed-ridden that those who remembered him at all thought of him as a man who had died a long time ago.

'There's nothing else for it,' said one of the twins, leaving down his spade, and immediately the other twin laid his spade beside it.

The two ancients on the headstones said nothing. Not even *they* could raise a voice against the possibilities of Malachi Roohan, the cooper. By their terrible aged silence they gave consent, and the widow turned to walk out of Cloon na Morav. One of the grave-diggers took out his pipe. The eyes of the other followed the widow, he hesitated, then walked after her. She became conscious of the man's step behind her as she got upon the stile, and turned her palely sad face upon him. He stood awkwardly, his eyes wandering, then said:

'Ask Malachi Roohan where the grave is, the exact place.'

It was to do this the widow was leaving Cloon na Morav; she had just announced that she was going to ask Malachi Roohan where the grave was. Yet the man's tone was that of one who was giving her extraordinarily acute advice. There was a little half-embarrassed note of confidence in his tone. In a dim way the widow thought that, maybe, he had accompanied her to the stile in a little awkward impulse of sympathy. Men were very curious in their ways sometimes. The widow was a very well-mannered woman, and she tried to look as if she had received a very valuable direction. She said:

'I will. I'll put that question to Malachi Roohan.'

And then she passed out over the stile.

III

The widow went up the road, and beyond it struck the first of the houses of the nearby town. She passed through faded streets in her quiet gait, moderately grief-stricken at the death of her weaver. She had been his fourth wife, and the widowhoods of fourth wives have not the rich abandon, the great emotional cataclysm, of first, or even second, widowhoods. It is a little chastened in its poignancy. The widow had a nice feeling that it would be out of place to give way to any of the characteristic manifestations of normal widowhood. She shrank from drawing attention to the fact that she had been a fourth wife. People's memories become so extraordinarily acute to family history in times of death! The widow did not care to come in as a sort of dramatic surprise in the gossip of the people about the weaver's life. She had heard snatches of such gossip at the wake the night before. She was beginning to understand why people love wakes and the intimate personalities of wakehouses. People listen to, remember, and believe what they hear at wakes. It is more precious to them than anything they ever hear in school, church, or playhouse. It is hardly because they get certain entertainment at the wake. It is more because the wake is a grand review of family ghosts. There one hears all the stories, the little flattering touches, the little unflattering bitternesses, the traditions, the astonishing records, of the clans. The woman with a memory speaking to the company from a chair beside a laid-out corpse carries more authority than the bishop allocuting from his chair. The wake is realism. The widow had heard a great deal at the wake about the clan of the weavers, and noted, without expressing any emotion, that she had come into the story not like other women, for anything personal to her own womanhood — for beauty, or high spirit, or temper, or faithfulness, or unfaithfulness — but simply because she was a fourth wife, a kind of curiosity, the back-wash of Mortimer Hehir's romances. The widow felt a remote sense of injustice in all this. She had said to herself that widows who had been fourth wives deserved more sympathy than widows who had been first wives, for the simple reason that fourth widows had never been, and could never be, first wives! The thought confused her a little, and she did not pursue it, instinctively feeling that if she did accept the conventional view of her condition she would only crystallize her widowhood into a grievance that nobody would try to understand, and which would, accordingly, be merely useless. And what was the good of it, anyhow? The widow smoothed her dark hair on each side of her head under her shawl.

She had no bitter and no sweet memories of the weaver. There was nothing that was even vivid in their marriage. She had no complaints to make of Mortimer Hehir. He had not come to her in any fiery love impulse. It was the marriage of an old man with a woman years younger. She had recognized him as an old man from first to last, a man who had already been thrice through a wedded experience, and her temperament, naturally calm, had met his half-stormy, half-petulant character, without suffering any sort of shock. The weaver had tried to keep up to the illusion of a perennial youth by dyeing his hair, and marrying one wife as soon as possible after another. The fourth wife had come to him late in life. She had a placid understanding that she was a mere flattery to the weaver's truculent egoism.

These thoughts, in some shape or other, occupied, without agitating, the mind of the widow as she passed, a dark shadowy figure through streets that were clamorous in their quietudes, painful in their lack of all the purposes for which streets have ever been created. Her only emotion was one which she knew to be quite creditable to her situation: a sincere desire to see the weaver buried in the grave to which the respectability of his family and the claims of his ancient house fully and fairly entitled him. The proceedings in Cloon na Morav had been painful, even tragical, to the widow. The weavers had always been great authorities and zealous guardians of the ancient burial place. This function had been traditional and voluntary with them. This was especially true of the last of them, Mortimer Hehir. He had been the greatest of all authorities on the burial places of the local clans. His knowledge was scientific. He had been the grand savant of Cloon na Morav. He had policed the place. Nay, he had been its tyrant. He had over and over again prevented terrible mistakes, complications that would have appalled those concerned if they were not beyond all such concerns. The widow of the weaver had often thought that in his day Mortimer Hehir had made his solicitation for the place a passion, unreasonable, almost violent. They said that all this had sprung from a fear that had come to him in his early youth that through some blunder an alien, an inferior, even an enemy, might come to find his way into the family burial place of the weavers. This fear had made him what he was. And in his later years his pride in the family burial place became a worship. His trade had gone down, and his pride had gone up. The burial ground in Cloon na Morav was the grand proof of his aristocracy. That was the coat-of-arms, the estate, the mark of high breeding, in the weavers. And now the man who had minded everybody's grave had not been able to mind his own. The widow thought that it was one of those injustices which blacken the reputation of the whole earth. She had felt, indeed, that she had been herself slack not to have learned long ago the lie of this precious grave from the weaver himself; and that he himself had been slack in not properly instructing her. But that was the way in this miserable world! In his passion for classifying the rights of others, the weaver had obscured his own. In his long and entirely successful battle in keeping alien corpses out of his own aristocratic pit he had made his own corpse alien to every pit in the place. The living high priest was the dead pariah of Cloon na Morav. Nobody could now tell except, perhaps, Malachi Roohan, the precise spot which he had defended against the blunders and confusions of the entire community, a dead-forgetting, indifferent, slack lot!

The widow tried to recall all she had ever heard the weaver

say about his grave, in the hope of getting some clue, something that might be better than the scandalous scatter-brained efforts of Meehaul Lynskey and Cahir Bowes. She remembered various detached things that the weaver, a talkative man, had said about his grave. Fifty years ago since that grave had been last opened, and it had then been opened to receive the remains of his father. It had been thirty years previous to that since it had taken in his father, that is, the newly dead weaver's father's father. The weavers were a long-lived lot, and there were not many males of them; one son was as much as any one of them begot to pass to the succession of the loom; if there were daughters they scattered, and their graves were continents apart. The three wives of the late weaver were buried in the new cemetery. The widow remembered that the weaver seldom spoke of them, and took no interest in their resting place. His heart was in Cloon na Morav and the sweet, dry, deep, aristocratic bed he had there in reserve for himself. But all his talk had been generalization. He had never, that the widow could recall, said anything about the site, about the signs and measurements by which it could be identified. No doubt, it had been well known to many people, but they had all died. The weaver had never realized what their slipping away might mean to himself. The position of the grave was so intimate to his own mind that it never occurred to him that it could be obscure to the minds of others. Mortimer Hehir had passed away like some learned and solitary astronomer who had discovered a new star, hugging its beauty, its exclusiveness, its possession to his heart, secretly rejoicing how its name would travel with his own through heavenly space for all time — and forgetting to mark its place among the known stars grouped upon his charts. Meehaul Lynskey and Cahir Bowes might now be two seasoned astronomers of venal knowledge looking for the star which the weaver, in his love for it, had let slip upon the mighty complexity of the skies.

The thing that is clearest to the mind of a man is often the thing that is most opaque to the intelligence of his bosom companion. A saint may walk the earth in the simple belief that all the world beholds his glowing halo; but all the world does not; if it did the saint would be stoned. And Mortimer Hehir had been as innocently proud of his grave as a saint might be ecstatic of his halo. He believed that when the time came he would get a royal funeral — a funeral fitting to the last of the line of great Cloon na Morav weavers. Instead of that they had no more idea of where to bury him than if he had been a wild tinker of the roads.

The widow, thinking of these things in her own mind, was about to sigh when, behind a window pane, she heard the sudden bubble of a roller canary's song. She had reached, half absent-mindedly, the home of Malachi Roohan, the cooper.

IV

The widow of the weaver approached the door of Malachi Roohan's house with an apologetic step, pawing the threshold a little in the manner of peasant women — a mannerism picked up from shy animals — before she stooped her head and made her entrance.

Malachi Roohan's daughter withdrew from the fire a face which reflected the passionate soul of a cook. The face cooled as the widow disclosed her business.

'I wouldn't put it a-past my father to have knowledge of the grave,' said the daughter of the house, adding, 'The Lord a mercy on the weaver.'

She led the widow into the presence of the cooper.

The room was small and low and stuffy, indifferently served with light by an unopenable window. There was the smell of old age, of decay, in the room. It brought almost a sense of faintness to the widow. She had the feeling that God had made her to move in the ways of old men — passionate, cantankerous, egoistic old men, old men for whom she was always doing something, always remembering things, from missing buttons to lost graves.

Her eyes sought the bed of Malachi Roohan with an unemotional, quietly sceptical gaze. But she did not see anything of the cooper. The daughter leaned over the bed, listened attentively, and then very deftly turned down the clothes, revealing the bust of Malachi Roohan. The widow saw a weird face, not in the least pale or lined, but ruddy, with a mahogany bald head, a head upon which the leathery skin — for there did not seem any flesh — hardly concealed the stark outlines of the skull. From the chin there strayed a grey beard, the most shaken and whipped-looking beard that the widow had ever seen; it was, in truth, a very miracle of a beard, for one wondered how it had come there, and having come there, how it continued to hang on, for there did not seem anything to which it could claim natural allegiance. The widow was as much astonished at this beard as if she saw a plant growing in a pot without soil. Through its gaps she could see the leather of the skin, the bones of a neck, which was indeed a neck. Over this head and shoulders the cooper's daughter bent and shouted into a crumpled ear. A little spasm of life stirred in the mummy. A low, mumbling sound came from the bed. The widow was already beginning to feel that, perhaps, she had done wrong in remembering that the cooper was still extant. But what else could she have done? If the weaver was buried in a wrong grave she did not believe that his soul would ever rest in peace. And what could be more dreadful than a soul wandering on the howling winds of the earth? The weaver would grieve, even in heaven, for his grave, grieve, maybe, as bitterly as a saint might grieve who had lost his halo. He was a passionate old man, such an old man as would have a turbulent spirit. He would surely —. The widow stifled the thoughts that flashed into her mind. She was no more superstitious than the rest of us, but —. These vague and terrible fears, and her moderately decent sorrow, were alike banished from her mind by what followed. The mummy on the bed came to life. And, what was more, he did it himself.

His daughter looked on with the air of one whose sensibilities had become blunted by a long familiarity with the various stages of his resurrections. The widow gathered that the daughter had been well drilled; she had been taught how to keep her place. She did not tender the slightest help to her father as he drew himself together on the bed. He turned over on his side, then on his back, and stealthily began to insinuate his shoulder blades on the pillow, pushing up his weird head to the streak of light from the little window. The widow had been so long accustomed to assist the aged that she made some involuntary movement of succour. Some half-seen gesture by the daughter, a sudden lifting of the eyelids on the face of the patient, disclosing a pair of blue eyes, gave the widow instinctive pause. She remained where she was, aloof like the daughter of the house. And as she caught the blue of Malachi Roohan's eyes it broke upon the widow that here in the essence of the cooper there lived a spirit of extraordinary independence. Here, surely, was a man who had been accustomed to look out for himself, who resented the attentions, even in these days of his flickering consciousness. Up he wormed his shoulder blades, his mahogany skull, his leathery skin, his sensational eyes, his miraculous beard, to the light and to the full view of the visitor. At a certain stage of the resurrection — when the cooper had drawn two long, stringy arms from under the clothes — his daughter made a drilled movement forward, seeking something in the bed. The widow saw her discover the end of a rope, and this she placed in the hands of her indomitable father. The other end of the rope was fastened to the iron rail at the foot of the bed. The sinews of the patient's hands clutched the rope, and slowly, wonderfully, magically, as it seemed to the widow, the cooper raised himself to a sitting posture in the bed. There was dead silence in the room except for the laboured breathing of the performer. The eyes of the widow blinked. Yes, there was that ghost of a man hoisting himself up from the dead on a length of rope reversing the usual procedure. By that length of rope did the cooper hang on to life, and the effort of life. It represented his connection with the world, the world which had forgotten him, which marched past his window outside without knowing the stupendous thing that went on in his room. There he was, sitting up in the bed, restored to view by his own unaided efforts, holding his grip on life to the last. It cost him something to do it, but he did it. It would take him longer and longer every day to grip along that length of rope; he would fail ell by ell, sinking back to the last helplessness on his rope, descending into eternity as a vessel is lowered on a rope into a dark, deep well. But there he was now, still able for his work, unbeholding to all, self-dependent and alive, looking a little vaguely with his blue eyes at the widow of the weaver. His daughter swiftly and quietly propped pillows at his back, and she did it with the air of one who was allowed a special privilege.

'Nan!' called the old man to his daughter.

The widow, cool-tempered as she was, almost jumped on her feet. The voice was amazingly powerful. It was like a shout, filling the little room with vibrations. For four things did the widow ever after remember Malachi Roohan — for his rope, his blue eyes, his powerful voice, and his magic beard. They were thrown on the background of his skeleton in powerful relief.

'Yes, Father,' his daughter replied, shouting into his ear. He was apparently very deaf. This infirmity came upon the widow with a shock. The cooper was full of physical surprises.

'Who's this one?' the cooper shouted, looking at the widow. He had the belief that he was delivering an aside.

'Mrs. Hehir.'

'Mrs. Hehir — what Hehir would she be?'

'The weaver's wife.'

'The weaver? Is it Mortimer Hehir?'

'Yes, Father.'

'In troth I know her. She's Delia Morrissey, that married the weaver; Delia Morrissey that he followed to Munster, a raving lunatic with the dint of love.'

A hot wave of embarrassment swept the widow. For a moment she thought the mind of the cooper was wandering. Then she remembered that the maiden name of the weaver's first wife was, indeed, Delia Morrissey. She had heard it, by chance, once or twice.

'Isn't it Delia Morrissey herself we have in it?' the old man asked.

The widow whispered to the daughter:

'Leave it so.'

She shrank from a difficult discussion with the spectre on the bed on the family history of the weaver. A sense of shame came to her that she could be the wife to a contemporary of this astonishing old man holding on to the life-rope.

'I'm out!' shouted Malachi Roohan, his blue eyes lighting suddenly. 'Delia Morrissey died. She was one day eating her dinner and a bone stuck in her throat. The weaver clapped her on the back, but it was all to no good. She choked to death before his eyes on the floor. I remember that. And the weaver himself near died of grief after. But he married secondly. Who's this he married secondly, Nan?'

Nan did not know. She turned to the widow for enlightenment. The widow moistened her lips. She had to concentrate her thoughts on a subject which, for her own peace of mind, she had habitually avoided. She hated genealogy. She said a little nervously:

'Sara MacCabe.'

The cooper's daughter shouted the name into his ear.

'So you're Sally MacCabe, from Looscaun, the one Mortimer took off the blacksmith? Well, well, that was a great business surely, the pair of them hot-tempered men, and your own beauty going to their heads like strong drink.'

He looked at the widow, a half-sceptical, half-admiring expression flickering across the leathery face. It was such a look as he might have given to Dergorvilla of Leinster, Deirdre of Uladh, or Helen of Troy.

The widow was not the notorious Sara MacCabe from

Looscaun; that lady had been the second wife of the weaver. It was said they had led a stormy life, made up of passionate quarrels and partings, and still more passionate reconciliations, Sara MacCabe from Looscaun not having quite forgotten or wholly neglected the blacksmith after her marriage to the weaver. But the widow again only whispered to the cooper's daughter:

'Leave it so.'

'What way is Mortimer keeping?' asked the old man.

'He's dead,' replied the daughter.

The fingers of the old man quivered on the rope.

'Dead? Mortimer Hehir dead?' he cried. 'What in the name of God happened him?'

Nan did not know what happened him. She knew that the widow would not mind, so, without waiting for a prompt, she replied:

'A weakness came over him, a sudden weakness.'

'To think of a man being whipped off all of a sudden like that!' cried the cooper. 'When that's the way it was with Mortimer Hehir what one of us can be sure at all? Nan, none of us is sure! To think of the weaver, with his heart as strong as a bull, going off in a little weakness! It's the treacherous world we live in, the treacherous world, surely. Never another yard of tweed will he put up on his old loom! Morty, Morty, you were a good companion, a great warrant to walk the hills, whistling the tunes, pleasant in your conversation and as broad-spoken as the Bible.'

'Did you know the weaver well, Father?' the daughter asked.

'Who better?' he replied, 'Who drank more pints with him than what myself did? And indeed it's to his wake I'd be setting out, and it's under his coffin my shoulder would be going, if I wasn't confined to my rope.'

He bowed his head for a few moments. The two women exchanged a quick, sympathetic glance.

The breathing of the old man was the breathing of one who slept. The head sank lower.

The widow said:

'You ought to make him lie down. He's tired.'

The daughter made some movement of dissent; she was afraid to interfere. Maybe the cooper could be very violent if roused. After a time he raised his head again. He looked in a new mood. He was fresher, more wide-awake. His beard hung in wisps to the bedclothes.

'Ask him about the grave,' the widow said.

The daughter hesitated a moment, and in that moment the cooper looked up as if he had heard, or partially heard. He said:

'If you wait a minute now I'll tell you what the weaver was.' He stared for some seconds at the little window.

'Oh, we'll wait,' said the daughter, and turning to the widow, added, 'won't we, Mrs. Hehir?'

'Indeed we will wait,' said the widow.

'The weaver,' said the old man suddenly, 'was a dream.'

He turned his head to the women to see how they had taken it.

'Maybe,' said the daughter, with a little touch of laughter, 'maybe Mrs. Hehir would not give in to that.'

The widow moved her hands uneasily under her shawl. She stared a little fearfully at the cooper. His blue eyes were clear as lake water over white sand.

'Whether she gives in to it, or whether she doesn't give in to it,' said Malachi Roohan, 'it's a dream Mortimer Hehir was. And his loom, and his shuttles, and his warping bars, and his bonnin, and the threads that he put upon the shifting racks, were all a dream. And the only thing he ever wove upon his loom was a dream.'

The old man smacked his lips, his hard gums whacking. His daughter looked at him with her head a little to one side.

'And what's more,' said the cooper, 'every woman that ever came into his head, and every wife he married, was a dream. I'm telling you that, Nan, and I'm telling it to you of the weaver. His life was a dream, and his death is a dream. And his widow there is a dream. And all the world is a dream. Do you hear me, Nan, this world is all a dream.'

'I hear you very well, Father,' the daughter sang in a piercing voice.

The cooper raised his head with a jerk, and his beard swept forward, giving him an appearance of vivid energy. He spoke in a voice like a trumpet blast:

'And I'm a dream!'

He turned his blue eyes on the widow. An unnerving sensation came to her. The cooper was the most dreadful old man she had ever seen, and what he was saying sounded the most terrible thing she had ever listened to. He cried:

'The idiot laughing in the street, the king looking at his crown, the woman turning her head to the sound of a man's step, the bells ringing in the belfry, the man walking his land, the weaver at his loom, the cooper handling his barrel, the Pope stooping for his red slippers — they're all a dream. And I'll tell you why they're a dream: because this world was meant to be a dream.'

'Father,' said the daughter, 'you're talking too much. You'll over-reach yourself.'

The old man gave himself a little pull on the rope. It was his gesture of energy, a demonstration of the fine fettle he was in. He said:

'You're saying that because you don't understand me.'

'I understand you very well.'

'You only think you do. Listen to me now, Nan. I want you to do something for me. You won't refuse me?'

'I will not refuse you, Father; you know very well I won't.'

'You're a good daughter to me, surely, Nan. And do what I tell you now. Shut close your eyes. Shut them fast and tight. No fluttering of the lids now.'

'Very well, Father.'

The daughter closed her eyes, throwing up her face in the attitude of one blind. The widow was conscious of the woman's strong, rough features, something good-natured in the line of the large mouth. The old man watched the face of his daughter with excitement. He asked:

'What is that you see now, Nan?'

'Nothing at all, Father.'

'In troth you do. Keep them closed tight and you'll see it.'

'I see nothing only——'

'Only what? Why don't you say it?'

'Only darkness, Father.'

'And isn't that something to see? Isn't it easier to see darkness than to see light? Now, Nan, look into the darkness.'

'I'm looking, Father.'

'And think of something — anything at all — the stool before the kitchen fire outside.'

'I'm thinking of it.'

'And do you remember it?'

'I do well.'

'And when you remember it what do you want to do — sit on it, maybe?'

'No, Father.'

'And why wouldn't you want to sit on it?'

'Because — because I'd like to see it first, to make sure.'

The old man gave a little crow of delight. He cried:

'There it is! You want to make sure that it is there, although you remember it well. And that is the way with everything in this world. People close their eyes and they are not sure of anything. They want to see it again before they believe. There is Nan, now, and she does not believe in the stool before the fire, the little stool she's looking at all her life, that her mother used to seat her on before the fire when she was a small child. She closes her eyes, and it is gone! And listen to me now, Nan — if you had a man of your own and you closed your eyes you wouldn't be too sure he was the man you remembered, and you'd want to open your eyes and look at him to make sure he was the man you knew before the lids dropped on your eyes. And if you had children about you and you turned your back and closed your eyes and tried to remember them you'd want to look at them to make sure. You'd be no more sure of them than you are now of the stool in the kitchen. One flash of the eyelids and everything in this world is gone.

'I'm telling you, Father, you're talking too much.'

'I'm not talking half enough. Aren't we all uneasy about the world, the things in the world that we can only believe in while we're looking at them? From one season of our life to another haven't we a kind of belief that some time we'll waken up and find everything different? Didn't you ever feel that, Nan? Didn't you think things would change, that the world would be a new place altogether, and that all that was going on around us was only a business that was doing us out of something else? We put up with it while the little hankering is nibbling at the butt of our hearts for the something else! All the men there be who believe that some day The Thing will happen, that they'll turn round the corner and waken up in the new great Street!'

'And sure,' said the daughter, 'maybe they are right, and maybe they will waken up.'

The old man's body was shaken with a queer spasm of laughter. It began under the clothes on the bed, worked up his trunk, ran along his stringy arms, out into the rope, and the iron foot of the bed rattled. A look of extraordinarily malicious humour lit up the vivid face of the cooper. The widow beheld him with fascination, a growing sense of alarm. He might say anything. He might do anything. He might begin to sing some fearful song. He might leap out of bed.

'Nan,' he said, 'do you believe you'll swing round the corner and waken up?'

'Well,' said Nan, hesitating a little, 'I do.'

The cooper gave a sort of peacock crow again. He cried:

'Och! Nan Roohan believes she'll waken up! Waken up from what? From a sleep and from a dream, from this world! Well, if you believe that, Nan Roohan, it shows you know what's what. You know what the thing around you, called the world, is. And it's only dreamers who can hope to waken up — do you hear me, Nan; it's only dreamers who can hope to waken up.'

'I hear you,' said Nan.

'The world is only a dream, and a dream is nothing at all! We all want to waken up out of the great nothingness of this world.'

'And, please God, we will,' said Nan.

'You can tell all the world from me,' said the cooper, 'that we won't.'

'And why won't we, Father?'

'Because,' said the old man, 'we ourselves are the dream. When we're over the dream is over with us. That's why.'

'Father,' said the daughter, her head again a little to one side, 'you know a great deal.'

'I know enough,' said the cooper shortly.

'And maybe you could tell us something about the weaver's grave. Mrs. Hehir wants to know.'

'And amn't I after telling you all about the weaver's grave? Amn't I telling you it is all a dream?'

'You never said that, Father. Indeed you never did.'

'I said everything in this world is a dream, and the weaver's grave is in this world, below in Cloon na Morav.'

'Where in Cloon na Morav? What part of it, Father? That is what Mrs. Hehir wants to know. Can you tell her?'

'I can tell her,' said Malachi Roohan. 'I was at his father's burial. I remember it above all burials, because that was the day the handsome girl, Honor Costello, fell over a grave and fainted. The sweat broke out on young Donohoe when he saw Honor Costello tumbling over the grave. Not a marry would he marry her after that, and he sworn to it by the kiss of her lips. "I'll marry no woman that fell on a grave," says Donohoe. "She'd maybe have a child by me with turned-in eyes or a twisted limb." So he married a farmer's daughter, and the same morning Honor Costello married a cattle drover. Very well, then. Donohoe's wife had no child at all. She was a barren woman. Do you hear me, Nan? A barren woman she was. And such childer as Honor Costello had by the drover! Yellow hair they had, heavy as seaweed, the skin of them clear as the wind, and limbs as clean as a whistle! It was said the drover was of the blood of the Danes, and it broke out in Honor Costello's family!'

'Maybe,' said the daughter, 'they were Vikings.'

'What are you saying?' cried the old man testily. 'Ain't I telling you it's Danes they were. Did any one ever hear a greater miracle.

'No one ever did,' said the daughter, and both women clicked their tongues to express sympathetic wonder at the tale.

'And I'll tell you what saved Honor Costello,' said the cooper. 'When she fell in Cloon na Morav she turned her cloak inside out.'

'What about the weaver's grave, Father? Mrs. Hehir wants to know.'

The old man looked at the widow; his blue eyes searched her face and her figure; the expression of satirical admiration flashed over his features. The nostrils of the nose twitched. He said:

'So that's the end of the story! Sally MacCabe, the blacksmith's favourite, wants to know where she'll sink the weaver out of sight! Great battles were fought in Looscaun over Sally MacCabe! The weaver thought his heart would burst, and the blacksmith damned his soul for the sake of Sally MacCabe's idle hours.'

'Father,' said the daughter of the house, 'let the dead rest.'

'Aye,' said Malachi Roohan, 'let the foolish dead rest. The dream of Looscaun is over. And now the pale woman is looking for the black weaver's grave. Well, good luck to her!'

The cooper was taken with another spasm of grotesque laughter. The only difference was that this time it began by the rattling of the rail of the bed, travelled along the rope, down his stringy arms dying out somewhere in his legs in the bed. He smacked his lips, a peculiar harsh sound, as if there was not much meat to it.

'Do I know where Mortimer Hehir's grave is?' he said ruminatingly. 'Do I know where me rope is?'

'Where is it, then?' his daughter asked. Her patience was great.

'I'll tell you that,' said the cooper. 'It's under the elm tree of Cloon na Morav. That's where it is surely. There was never a weaver yet that did not find rest under the elm tree of Cloon na Morav. There they all went as surely as the buds came on the branches. Let Sally MacCabe put poor Morty there; let her give him a tear or two in memory of the days that his heart was ready to burst for her, and believe you me no ghost will ever haunt her. No dead man ever yet came back to look upon a woman!'

A furtive sigh escaped the widow. With her handkerchief she wiped a little perspiration from both sides of her nose. The old man wagged his head sympathetically. He thought she was the long dead Sally MacCabe lamenting the weaver! The widow's emotion arose from relief that the mystery of the grave had at last been cleared up. Yet her dealings with old men had taught her caution. Quite suddenly the memory of the handsome dark face of the grave-digger who had followed her to the stile came back to her. She remembered that he said something about 'the exact position of the grave.' The widow prompted yet another question:

'What position under the elm tree?'

'The old man listened to the question; a strained look came into his face.

'Position of what?' he asked.

'Of the grave?'

'Of what grave?'

'The weaver's grave.'

Another spasm seized the old frame, but this time it came from no aged merriment. It gripped his skeleton and shook it. It was as if some invisible powerful hand had suddenly taken him by the back of the neck and shaken him. His knuckles rattled on the rope. They had an appalling sound. A horrible feeling came to the widow that the cooper would fall to pieces like a bag of bones. He turned his face to his daughter. Great tears had welled into the blue eyes, giving them an appearance of childish petulance, then of acute suffering.

'What are you talking to me of graves for?' he asked, and the powerful voice broke. 'Why will you be tormenting me like this? It's not going to die I am, is it? Is it going to die I am, Nan?'

The daughter bent over him as she might bend over a child. She said:

'Indeed, there's great fear of you. Lie down and rest yourself. Fatigued out and out you are.'

The grip slowly slackened on the rope. He sank back, quite helpless, a little whimper breaking from him. The daughter stooped lower, reaching for a pillow that had fallen in by the wall. A sudden sharp snarl sounded from the bed, and it dropped from her hand.

'Don't touch me!' the cooper cried. The voice was again restored, powerful in its command. And to the amazement of the widow she saw him again grip along the rope and rise in the bed.

'Amn't I tired telling you not to touch me?' he cried. 'Have I any business talking to you at all? Is it gone my authority is in this house?'

He glared at his daughter, his eyes red with anger, like a dog crouching in his kennel, and the daughter stepped back, a wry smile on her large mouth. The widow stepped back with her, and for a moment he held the women with their backs to the wall by his angry red eyes. Another growl and the cooper sank back inch by inch on the rope. In all her experience of old men the widow had never seen anything like this old man; his resurrections and his collapse. When he was quite down the daughter gingerly put the clothes over his shoulders and then beckoned the widow out of the room.

The widow left the house of Malachi Roohan, the cooper, with the feeling that she had discovered the grave of an old man by almost killing another.

V

The widow walked along the streets, outwardly calm, inwardly confused. Her first thought was 'the day is going on me!' There were many things still to be done at home; she remembered the weaver lying there, quiet at last, the candles lighting about him, the brown habit over him, a crucifix in his hands — everything as it should be. It seemed ages to the widow since he had really fallen ill. He was very exacting and peevish all that time. His death agony had been protracted, almost melodramatically violent. A few times the widow had nearly run out of the house, leaving the weaver to fight the death battle alone. But her common sense, her good nerves, and her religious convictions had stood to her, and when she put the pennies on the weaver's eyes she was glad she had done her duty to the last. She was glad now that she had taken the search for the grave out of the hands of Meehaul Lynskey and Cahir Bowes; Malachi Roohan had been a sight, and she would never forget him, but he had known what nobody else knew. The widow, as she ascended a little upward sweep of the road to Cloon na Morav, noted that the sky beyond it was more vivid, a red band of light having struck across the grey-blue, just on the horizon. Up against this red background was the dark outline of landscape, and especially Cloon na Morav. She kept her eyes upon it as she drew nearer. Objects that were vague on the landscape began to bulk up with more distinction.

She noted the back wall of Cloon na Morav, its green lichen more vivid under the red patch of the skyline. And presently, above the green wall, black against the vivid sky, she saw elevated the bulk of one of the black cockroaches. On it were perched two drab figures, so grotesque, so still, that they seemed part of the thing itself. One figure was sloping out from the end of the tombstone so curiously that for a moment the widow thought it was a man who had reached down from the table to see what was under it. At the other end of the table was a slender warped figure, and as the widow gazed upon it she saw a sign of animation. The head and face, bleak in their outlines, were raised up in a gesture of despair. The face was turned flush against the sky, so much so that the widow's eyes instinctively sought the sky too. Above the slash of red, in the west, was a single star, flashing so briskly and so freshly that it might have never shone before. For all the widow knew, it might have been a young star frolicking in the heavens with all the joy of youth. Was that, she wondered, at what the old man, Meehaul Lynskey, was gazing. He was very, very old, and the star was very, very young! Was there some protest in the gesture of the head he raised to that thing in the sky; was there some mockery in the sparkle of the thing of the sky for the face of the man? Why should a star be always young, a man aged so soon? Should not a man be greater than a star? Was it this Meehaul Lynskey was thinking? The widow could not say, but something in the thing awed her. She had the sensation of one who surprises a man in some act that lifts him above the commonplaces of existence. It was as if Meehaul Lynskey were discovered prostrate before some altar, in the throes of a religious agony. Old men were, the widow felt, very, very strange, and she did not know that she would ever understand them. As she looked at the bleak head of Meehaul Lynskey up against the vivid patch of the sky, she wondered if there could really be something in that head which would make him as great as a star, immortal as a star? Suddenly Meehaul Lynskey made a movement. The widow saw it quite distinctly. She saw the arm raised, the hand go out, with its crooked fingers, in one, two, three quick, short taps in the direction of the star. The widow stood to watch, and the gesture was so familiar, so homely, so personal, that it was quite understandable to her. She knew then that Meehaul Lynskey was not thinking of any great things at all. He was only a nailer! And seeing the

Evening Star sparkle in the sky he had only thought of his workshop, of the bellows, the irons, the fire, the sparks, and the glowing iron which might be made into a nail while it was hot! He had in imagination seized a hammer and made a blow across interstellar space at Venus! All the beauty and youth of the star frolicking on the pale sky above the slash of vivid redness had only suggested to him the making of yet another nail! If Meehaul Lynskey could push up his scarred yellow face among the stars of the sky he would only see in them the sparks of his little smithy.

Cahir Bowes was, the widow thought, looking down at the earth, from the other end of the tombstone, to see if there were any hard things there which he could smash up. The old men had their backs turned upon each other. Very likely they had had another discussion since, which ended in this attitude of mutual contempt. The widow was conscious again of the unreasonableness of old men, but not much resentful of it. She was too long accustomed to them to have any great sense of revolt. Her emotion, if it could be called an emotion, was a settled, dull toleration of all their little bigotries.

She put her hand on the stile for the second time that day, and again raised her palely sad face over the graveyard of Cloon na Morav. As she did so she had the most extraordinary experience of the whole day's sensations. It was such a sensation as gave her at once a wonderful sense of the reality and the unreality of life. She paused on the stile, and had a clear insight into something that had up to this moment been obscure. And no sooner had the thing become definite and clear than a sense of the wonder of life came to her. It was all very like the dream Malachi Roohan had talked about.

In the pale grass, under the vivid colours of the sky, the two grave-diggers were lying on their backs, staring silently up at the heavens. The widow looked at them as she paused on the stile. Her thoughts of these men had been indifferent, subconscious, up to this instant. They were handsome young men. Perhaps if there had been only one of them the widow would have been more attentive. The dark handsomeness did not seem the same thing when repeated. Their beauty, if one could call it beauty, had been collective, the beauty of flowers, of dark, velvety pansies, the distinctive marks of one faithfully duplicated on the other. The good looks of one had, to the mind of the widow, somehow nullified the good looks of the other. There was too much borrowing of Peter to pay Paul in their well-favoured features. The first grave-digger spoiled the illusion of individuality in the second grave-digger. The widow had not thought so, but she would have agreed if anybody whispered to her that a good-looking man who wanted to win favour with a woman should never have so complete a twin brother. It would be possible for a woman to part tenderly with a man, and, if she met his image and likeness around the corner, knock him down. There is nothing more powerful, but nothing more delicate in life than the valves of individuality. To create the impression that humanity was a thing which could be turned out like a coinage would be to ruin the whole illusion of life. The twin grave-diggers had created some sort of such impression, vague, and not very insistent, in the mind of the widow, and it had made her lose any special interest in them. Now, however, as she hesitated on the stile, all this was swept from her mind at a stroke. The most subtle and powerful of all things, personality, sprang silently from the twins and made them, to the mind of the widow, things as far apart as the poles. The two men lay at length, and exactly the same length and bulk, in the long, grey grass. But, as the widow looked upon them, one twin seemed conscious of her presence, while the other continued his absorption in the heavens above. The supreme twin turned his head, and his soft, velvety brown eyes met the eyes of the widow. There was welcome in the man's eyes. The widow read that welcome as plainly as if he had spoken his thoughts. The next moment he had sprung to his feet, smiling. He took a few steps forward, then, self-conscious, pulled up. If he had only jumped up and smiled the widow would have understood. But those few eager steps forward and then that stock stillness! The other twin rose reluctantly, and as he did so the widow was conscious of even physical differences in the brothers. The eyes were not the same. No such velvety soft lights were in the eyes of the second one. He was more sheepish. He was more phlegmatic. He was only a plagiarism of the original man! The widow wondered how she had not seen all this before. The resemblance between the twins was only skin deep. The two old men, at the moment the second twin rose, detached themselves slowly, almost painfully from their tombstone, and all moved forward to meet the widow. The widow, collecting her thoughts, piloted her skirts modestly about her legs as she got down from the narrow stonework of the stile and stumbled into the contrariness of Cloon na Morav. A wild sense of satisfaction swept her that she had come back the bearer of useful information.

'Well,' said Meehaul Lynskey, 'did you see Malachi Roohan?' The widow looked at his scorched, sceptical, yellow face, and said:

'I did.'

'Had he any word for us?'

'He had. He remembers the place of the weaver's grave.' The widow looked a little vaguely about Cloon na Morav.

'What does he say?'

'He says it's under the elm tree.'

There was silence. The stone-breaker swung about on his legs, his head making a semi-circular movement over the ground, and his sharp eyes were turned upward, as if he were searching the heavens for an elm tree. The nailer dropped his underjaw and stared tensely across the ground, blankly, patiently, like a fisherman on the edge of the shore gazing over an empty sea. The grave-digger turned his head away shyly, like a boy, as if he did not want to see the confusion of the widow; the man was full of the most delicate mannerisms. The other grave-digger settled into a stolid attitude, then the skin bunched up about his brown eyes in puckers of humour. A miserable feeling swept the widow. She had the feeling that she stood on the verge of some collapse.

'Under the elm tree,' mumbled the stone-breaker.

'That's what he said,' added the widow. 'Under the elm tree of Cloon na Morav.'

'Well,' said Cahir Bowes, 'when you find the elm tree you'll find the grave.'

The widow did not know what an elm tree was. Nothing had ever happened in life as she knew it to render any special knowledge of trees profitable, and therefore desirable. Trees were good; they made nice firing when chopped up; timber, and all that was fashioned out of timber, came from trees. This knowledge the widow had accepted as she had accepted all the other remote phenomena of the world into which she had been born. But that trees should have distinctive names, that they should have family relationships, seemed to the mind of the widow only an unnecessary complication of the affairs of the universe. What good was it? She could understand calling fruit trees fruit trees and all other kinds simply trees. But that one should be an elm and another an ash, that there should be name after name, species after species, giving them peculiarities and personalities, was one of the things that the widow did not like. And at this moment, when the elm tree of Malachi Roohan had raised a fresh problem in Cloon na Morav, the likeness of old men to old trees — their crankiness, their complexity, their angles, their very barks, bulges, gnarled twistiness, and kinks — was very close, and brought a sense of oppression to the sorely-tried brain of the widow.

'Under the elm tree,' repeated Meehaul Lynskey. 'The elm tree of Cloon na Morav.' He broke into an aged cackle of a laugh. 'If I was any good at all at making a rhyme I'd make one about that elm tree, devil a other but I would.'

The widow looked around Cloon na Morav, and her eyes for the first time in her life, were consciously searching for trees. If there were numerous trees there she could understand how easy it might be for Malachi Roohan to make a mistake. He might have mistaken some other sort of tree for an elm — the widow felt that there must be plenty of other trees very like an elm. In fact, she reasoned that other trees, do their best, could not help looking like an elm. There must be thousands and millions of people like herself in the world who pass through life in the belief that a certain kind of tree was an elm when, in reality, it may be an ash or an oak or a chestnut or a beech, or even a poplar, a birch, or a yew. Malachi Roohan was never likely to allow anybody to amend his knowledge of an elm tree. He would let go his rope in the belief that there was an elm tree in Cloon na Morav, and that under it was the weaver's grave — that is, if Malachi Roohan had not, in some ghastly aged kink, invented the thing. The widow, not sharply, but still with an appreciation of the thing, grasped that a dispute about trees would be the very sort of dispute in which Meehaul Lynskey and Cahir Bowes would, like the very old men that they were, have revelled. Under the impulse of the message she had brought from the cooper they would have launched out into another powerful struggle from tree to tree in Cloon na Morav; they would again have strewn the place with the corpses of slain arguments, and in the net result they would not have been able to establish anything either about elm trees or about the weaver's grave. The slow, sad gaze of the widow for trees in Cloon na Morav brought to her, in these circumstances, both pain and relief. It was a relief that Meehaul Lynskey and Cahir Bowes could not challenge each other to a battle of trees; it was a pain that the tree of Malachi Roohan was nowhere in sight. The widow could see for herself that there was not any sort of a tree in Cloon na Morav. The ground was enclosed upon three sides by walls, on the fourth by a hedge of quicks. Not even old men could transform a hedge into an elm tree. Neither could they make the few struggling briars clinging about the railings of the sepulchres into anything except briars. The elm tree of Malachi Roohan was now non-existent. Nobody would ever know whether it had or had not ever existed. The widow would as soon give the soul of the weaver to the howling winds of the world as go back and interview the cooper again on the subject.

'Old Malachi Roohan,' said Cahir Bowes with tolerant decision, 'is doting.'

'The nearest elm tree I know,' said Meehaul Lynskey, 'is half a mile away.'

'The one above at Carragh?' questioned Cahir Bowes.

'Aye, beside the mill.'

No more was to be said. The riddle of the weaver's grave was still the riddle of the weaver's grave. Cloon na Morav kept its secret. But, nevertheless, the weaver would have to be buried. He could not be housed indefinitely. Taking courage from all the harrowing aspects of the deadlock, Meehaul Lynskey went back, plump and courageously to his original allegiance.

'The grave of the weaver is there,' he said, and he struck out his hooked fingers in the direction of the disturbance of the sod which the grave-diggers had made under pressure of his earlier enthusiasm.

Cahir Bowes turned on him with a withering, quavering glance.

'Aren't you afraid that God would strike you where you stand?' he demanded.

'I'm not — not a bit afraid,' said Meehaul Lynskey. 'It's the weaver's grave.'

'You say that,' cried Cahir Bowes, 'after what we all saw and what we all heard?'

'I do,' said Meehaul Lynskey, stoutly. He wiped his lips with the palm of his hand, and launched out into one of his arguments, as usual, packed with particulars.

'I saw the weaver's father lowered in that place. And I'll tell you, what's more, it was Father Owen MacCarthy that read over him, he a young red-haired curate in this place at the time, long before ever he became parish priest of Benelog. There was I, standing in this exact spot, a young man, too, with a light moustache, holding me hat in me hand, and there one side of me — maybe five yards from the marble stone of the Keernahans — was Patsy Curtin that drank himself to death after, and on the other side of me was Honor Costello, that fell on the grave and married the cattle drover, a big, loose-shouldered Dane.'

Patiently, half absent-mindedly, listening to the renewal of the dispute, the widow remembered the words of Malachi Roohan, and his story of Honor Costello, who fell on the grave over fifty years ago. What memories these old men had! How unreliable they were, and yet flashing out astounding corroborations of each other. Maybe there was something in what Meehaul Lynskey was saying. Maybe — but the widow checked her thoughts. What was the use of it all? This grave could not be the weaver's grave; it had been grimly demonstrated to them all that it was full of stout coffins. The widow, with a gesture of agitation, smoothed her hair down the gentle slope of her head under the shawl. As she did so her eyes caught the eyes of the grave-digger; he was looking at her! He withdrew his eyes at once, and began to twitch the ends of his dark moustache with his fingers.

'If,' said Cahir Bowes, 'this be the grave of the weaver, what's Julia Rafferty doing in it? Answer me that, Meehaul Lynskey.'

'I don't know what's she doing in it, and what's more, I don't care. And believe you my word, many a queer thing happened in Cloon na Morav that had no right to happen in it. Julia Rafferty, maybe, isn't the only one that is where she had no right to be.'

'Maybe she isn't,' said Cahir Bowes, 'but it's there she is, anyhow, and I'm thinking it's there she's likely to stay.'

'If she's in the weaver's grave,' cried Meehaul Lynskey, 'what I say is, out with her!'

'Very well, then, Meehaul Lynskey. Let you yourself be the powerful man to deal with Julia Rafferty. But remember this, and remember it's my word, that touch one bone in this place and you touch all.'

'No fear at all have I to right a wrong. I'm no backslider when it comes to justice, and justice I'll see done among the living and the dead.'

'Go ahead, then, me hearty fellow. If Julia herself is in the wrong place somebody else must be in her own place, and you'll be following one rightment with another wrongment until in the end you'll go mad with the tangle of dead men's wrongs. That's the end that's in store for you, Meehaul Lynskey.'

Meehaul Lynskey spat on his fist and struck out with the hooked fingers. His blood was up.

'That I may be as dead as my father!' he began in a traditional oath, and at that Cahir Bowes gave a little cry and raised his stick with a battle flourish. They went up and down the dips of the ground, rising and falling on the waves of their anger, and the widow stood where she was, miserable and downhearted, her feet growing stone cold from the chilly dampness of the ground. The twin, who did not now count, took out his pipe and lit it, looking at the old men with a stolid gaze. The twin who now counted walked uneasily away, bit an end off a chunk of tobacco, and came to stand in the ground in a line with the widow, looking on with her several feet away; but again the widow was conscious of the man's growing sympathy.

'They're a nice pair of boyos, them two old lads,' he remarked to the widow. He turned his head to her. He was very handsome.

'Do you think they will find it?' she asked. Her voice was a little nervous, and the man shifted on his feet, nervously responsive.

'It's hard to say,' he said. 'You'd never know what to think. Two old lads, the like of them, do be very tricky.'

'God grant they'll get it,' said the widow.

'God grant,' said the grave-digger.

But they didn't. They only got exhausted as before, wheezing and coughing, and glaring at each other as they sat down on two mounds.

The grave-digger turned to the widow.

She was aware of the nice warmth of his brown eyes.

'Are you waking the weaver again tonight?' he asked.

'I am,' said the widow.

'Well, maybe some person — some old man or woman from the country — may turn up and be able to tell where the grave is. You could make inquiries.'

'Yes,' said the widow, but without any enthusiasm, 'I could make inquiries.'

The grave-digger hesitated for a moment, and said more sympathetically. 'We could all, maybe, make inquiries.' There was a softer personal note, a note of adventure, in the voice.

The widow turned her head to the man and smiled at him quite frankly.

'I'm beholding to you,' she said and then added with a little wounded sigh, 'Everyone is very good to me.'

The grave-digger twirled the ends of his moustache.

Cahir Bowes, who had heard, rose from his mound and said briskly, 'I'll agree to leave it at that.' His air was that of one who had made an extraordinary personal sacrifice. What he was really thinking was that he would have another great day of it with Meehaul Lynskey in Cloon na Morav tomorrow. He'd show that oul' fellow, Lynskey, what stuff Boweses were made of.

'And I'm not against it,' said Meehaul Lynskey. He took the tone of one who was never to be outdone in magnanimity. He was also thinking of another day of effort tomorrow, a day that would, please God, show the Boweses what the Lynskeys were like.

With that the party came straggling out of Cloon na Morav, the two old men first, the widow next, the grave-diggers waiting to put on their coats and light their pipes.

There was a little upward slope on the road to the town, and as the two old men took it the widow thought they looked very spent after their day. She wondered if Cahir Bowes would ever be able for that hill. She would give him a glass of whiskey at home, if there was any left in the bottle. Of the two, and as limp and slack as his body looked, Meehaul Lynskey appeared the better able for the hill. They walked together, that is to say, abreast, but they kept almost the width of the road between each other, as if this gulf expressed the breach of friendship between them on the head of the dispute about the weaver's grave. They had been making liars of each other all day, and they would, please God, make liars of each other all day tomorrow. The widow, understanding the meaning of this hostility, had a faint sense of amusement at the contrariness of old men. How could she tell what was passing in the head which Cahir Bowes hung, like a fuchsia drop, over the road? How could she know of the strange rise and fall of the thoughts, the little frets, the tempers, the faint humours, which chased each other there? Nobody — not even Cahir Bowes himself — could account for them. All the widow knew was that Cahir Bowes stood suddenly on the road. Something had happened in his brain, some old memory cell long dormant had become nascent, had a stir, a pulse, a flicker of warmth, of activity, and swiftly as a flash of lightning in the sky, a glow of lucidity lit up his memory. It was as if a searchlight had suddenly flooded the dark corners of his brain. The immediate physical effect on Cahir Bowes was to cause him to stand stark still on the road, Meehaul Lynskey going ahead without him. The widow saw Cahir Bowes pivot on his heels, his head, at the end of the horizontal body, swinging round like the movement of a hand on a runaway clock. Instead of pointing up the hill homeward the head pointed down the hill and back to Cloon na Morav. There followed the most extraordinary movements — shufflings, gyrations — that the widow had ever seen. Cahir Bowes wanted to run like mad away down the road. That was plain. And Cahir Bowes believed that he was running like mad away down the road. That was also evident. But what he actually did was to make little jumps on his feet, his stick rattling the ground in front, and each jump did not bring him an inch of ground.

He would have gone more rapidly in his normal shuffle. His efforts were like a terrible parody on the springs of a kangaroo. And Cahir Bowes, in a voice that was now more a scream than a cackle, was calling out unintelligible things. The widow, looking at him, paused in wonder, then over her face there came a relaxation, a colour, her eyes warmed, her expression lost its settled pensiveness, and all her body was shaken with uncontrollable laughter. Cahir Bowes passed her on the road in his fantastic leaps, his abortive buck-jumps, screaming and cracking his stick on the ground, his left hand still gripped tightly on the small of his back behind, a powerful brake on the small of his back.

Meehaul Lynskey turned back and his face was shaken with an aged emotion as he looked after the stone-breaker. Then he removed his hat and blessed himself.

'The cross of Christ between us and harm,' he exclaimed. 'Old Cahir Bowes has gone off his head at last. I thought there was something up with him all day. It was easily known there was something ugly working in his mind.'

The widow controlled her laughter and checked herself, making the sign of the Cross on her forehead, too. She said:

'God forgive me for laughing and the weaver with the habit but fresh upon him.'

The grave-digger who counted was coming out somewhat eagerly over the stile, but Cahir Bowes, flourishing his stick, beat him back again and then himself re-entered Cloon na Morav. He stumbled over the grass, now rising on a mound, now disappearing altogether in a dip of the ground, travelling in a giddy course like a hooker in a storm; again, for a long time, he remained submerged, showing, however, the eternal stick, his periscope, his indication to the world that he was about his business. In a level piece of ground, marked by stones with large mottled white marks upon them, he settled and cried out to all, and calling God to witness, that this surely was the weaver's grave. There was scepticism, hesitation, on the part of the grave-diggers, but after some parley, and because Cahir Bowes was so passionate, vehement, crying and shouting, dribbling water from the mouth, showing his yellow teeth, pouring sweat on his forehead, quivering on his legs, they began to dig carefully in the spot. The widow, at this, re-arranged the shawl on her head and entered Cloon na Morav, conscious, as she shuffled over the stile, that a pair of warm brown eyes were, for a moment, upon her movements and then withdrawn. She stood a little way back from the digging and awaited the result with a slightly more accelerated beating of the heart. The twins looked as if they were ready to strike something unexpected at any moment, digging carefully, and Cahir Bowes hung over the place, cackling and crowing, urging the men to swifter work. The earth sang up out of the ground, dark and rich in colour, gleaming like gold, in the deepening twilight in the place. Two feet, three feet, four feet of earth came up, the spades pushing through the earth in regular and powerful pushes, and still the coast was clear. Cahir Bowes trembled with excitement on his stick. Five feet of a pit yawned in the ancient ground. The spade work ceased. One of the grave-diggers looked up at Cahir Bowes and said:

'You hit the weaver's grave this time right enough. Not another grave in the place could be as free as this.'

The widow sighed a quick little sigh and looked at the face of the other grave-digger, hesitated, then allowed a remote smile of thankfulness to flit across her palely sad face. The eyes of the man wandered away over the darkening spaces of Cloon na Morav.

'I got the weaver's grave surely,' cried Cahir Bowes, his old face full of weird animation. If he had found the Philosopher's Stone he would only have broken it. But to find the weaver's grave was an accomplishment that would help him into a wisdom before which all his world would bow. He looked around triumphantly and said:

'Where is Meehaul Lynskey now; what will the people be saying at all about his attack on Julia Rafferty's grave? Julia will haunt him, and I'd sooner have any one at all haunting me than the ghost of Julia Rafferty. Where is Meehaul Lynskey now? Is it ashamed to show his liary face he is? And what talk had Malachi Roohan about an elm tree? Elm tree, indeed! If it's trees that is troubling him now let him climb up one of them and hang himself from it with his rope! Where is that old fellow, Meehaul Lynskey, and his rotten head? Where is he, I say? Let him come in here now to Cloon na Morav until I be showing him the weaver's grave, five feet down and not a rib or a knuckle in it, as clean and beautiful as the weaver ever wished it. Come in here, Meehaul Lynskey, until I hear the lies panting again in your yellow throat.'

He went in his extraordinary movement over the ground, making for the stile all the while talking.

Meehaul Lynskey had crouched behind the wall outside when Cahir Bowes led the diggers to the new site, his old face twisted in an attentive, almost agonizing emotion. He stood peeping over the wall, saying to himself:

'Whisht, will you! Don't mind that old madman. He hasn't it at all. I'm telling you he hasn't it. Whisht, will you! Let him dig away. They'll hit something in a minute. They'll level him when they find out. His brain has turned. Whisht, now, will you, and I'll have that rambling old lunatic, Cahir Bowes, in a minute. I'll leap in on him. I'll charge him before the world. I'll show him up. I'll take the gab out of him. I'll lacerate him. I'll lambaste him. Whisht, will you!'

But as the digging went on and the terrible cries of triumph arose inside Meehaul Lynskey's knees knocked together. His head bent level to the wall, yellow and grimacing, nerves twitching across it, a little yellow froth gathering at the corners of the mouth. When Cahir Bowes came beating for the stile Meehaul Lynskey rubbed one leg with the other, a little below the calf, and cried brokenly to himself:

'God in Heaven, he has it! He has the weaver's grave.'

He turned about and slunk along in the shadow of the wall up the hill, panting and broken. By the time Cahir Bowes had reached the stile Meehaul Lynskey's figure was shadowily dipping down over the crest of the road. A sharp cry from Cahir Bowes caused him to shrink out of sight like a dog at whom a weapon had been thrown.

The eyes of the grave-digger who did not now count followed the figure of Cahir Bowes as he moved to the stile. He laughed a little in amusement, then wiped his brow. He came up out of the grave. He turned to the widow and said:

'We're down five feet. Isn't that enough in which to sink the weaver in? Are you satisfied?'

The man spoke to her without any pretence at fine feeling. He addressed her as a fourth wife should be addressed. The widow was conscious but unresentful of the man's manner. She regarded him calmly and without any resentment. On her part there was no resentment either, no hypocrisy, no make-believe. Her unemotional eyes followed his action as he stuck his spade into the loose mould on the ground. A cry from Cahir Bowes distracted the man, he laughed again, and before the widow could make a reply he said:

'Old Cahir is great value. Come down until we hear him handling the nailer.'

He walked away down over the ground.

The widow was left alone with the other grave-digger. He drew himself up out of the pit with a sinuous movement of the body which the widow noted. He stood without a word beside the pile of heaving clay and looked across at the widow. She looked back at him and suddenly the silence became full of unspoken words, of flying, ringing emotions. The widow could see the dark green wall, above it the band of still-deepening red, above that the still more pallid grey sky, and directly over the man's head the gay frolicking of the fresh star in the sky. Cloon na Morav was flooded with a deep, vague light. The widow scented the fresh wind about her, the cool fragrance of the earth, and yet a warmth that was strangely beautiful. The light of the man's dark eyes was visible in the shadow which hid his face. The pile of earth beside him was like a vague shape of miniature bronze mountains. He stood with a stillness which was tense and dramatic. The widow thought that the world was strange, the sky extraordinary, the man's head against the red sky a wonder, a poem, above it the sparkle of the great young star. The widow knew that they would be left together like this for one minute, a minute which would be as a flash and as eternity. And she knew now that sooner or later this man would come to her and that she would welcome him. Below at the stile the voice of Cahir Bowes was cackling in its aged notes. Beyond this the stillness was the stillness of heaven and earth. Suddenly a sense of faintness came to the widow. The whole place swooned before her eyes. Never was this world so strange, so like the dream that Malachi Roohan had talked about. A movement in the figure of the man beside the heap of bronze had come to her as a warning, a fear, and a delight. She moved herself a little in response, made a step backward. The next instant she saw the figure of the man spring across the open black mouth of the weaver's grave to her.

A faint sound escaped her and then his breath was hot on her face, his mouth on her lips.

Half a minute later Cahir Bowes came shuffling back, followed by the twin.

'I'll bone him yet,' said Cahir Bowes. 'Never you fear I'll make that old nailer face me. I'll show him up at the weaver's wake tonight!'

The twin laughed behind him. He shook his head at his brother, who was standing a pace away from the widow. He said:

'Five feet.'

He looked into the grave and then looked at the widow, saying:

'Are you satisfied?'

There was silence for a second or two, and when she spoke the widow's voice was low but fresh, like the voice of a young girl. She said:

'I'm satisfied.'

Part Two

Michael and Mary

MARY had spent many days gathering wool from the whins on the headland. They were the bits of wool shed by the sheep before the shearing. When she had got a fleece that fitted the basket she took it down to the canal and washed it. When she had done washing it was a soft, white, silky fleece. She put it back in the brown sally basket, pressing it down with her long, delicate fingers. She had risen to go away, holding the basket against her waist, when her eyes followed the narrow neck of water that wound through the bog.

She could not follow the neck of yellow water very far. The light of day was failing. A haze hung over the great Bog of Allen that spread out level on all sides of her. The boat loomed out of the haze on the narrow neck of the canal water. It looked, at first, a long way off, and it seemed to come in a cloud. The soft rose light that mounted the sky caught the boat and burnished it like dull gold. It came leisurely, drawn by the one horse, looking like a Golden Barque in the twilight. Mary put her brown head a little to one side as she watched the easy motion of the boat. The horse drew himself along deliberately, the patient head going up and down with every heavy step. A crane rose from the bog, flapping two lazy wings across the wake of the boat, and, reaching its long neck before it, got lost in the haze.

The figure that swayed by the big arm of the tiller on *The Golden Barque* was vague and shapeless at first, but Mary felt her eyes following the slow movements of the body.

Mary thought it was very beautiful to sway every now and then by the arm of the tiller, steering a Golden Barque through the twilight.

Then she realized suddenly that the boat was much nearer than she had thought. She could see the figures of the men plainly, especially the slim figure by the tiller. She could trace the rope that slackened and stretched taut as it reached from the boat to the horse. Once it splashed the water, and there was a little sprout of silver. She noted the whip looped under the arm of the driver. Presently she could count every heavy step of the horse, and was struck by the great size of the shaggy fetlocks. But always her eyes went back to the figure by the tiller.

She moved back a little way to see *The Golden Barque* pass. It came from a strange, far-off world, and having traversed the bog went away into another unknown world. A red-faced man was sitting drowsily on the prow. Mary smiled and nodded to him, but he made no sign. He did not see her; perhaps he was asleep. The driver who walked beside the horse had his head stooped and his eyes on the ground. He did not look up as he passed. Mary saw his lips moving, and heard him mutter to himself; perhaps he was praying. He was a shrunken, mis-shaped little figure and kept step with the brute in the journey over the bog. But Mary felt the gaze of the man by the tiller upon her. She raised her eyes.

The light was uncertain and his peaked cap threw a shadow over his face. But the figure was lithe and youthful. He smiled as she looked up, for she caught a gleam of his teeth. Then the boat had passed. Mary did not smile in return. She had taken a step back and remained there quietly. Once he looked back and awkwardly touched his cap, but she made no sign.

When the boat had gone by some way she sat down on the bank, her basket of wool beside her, looking at *The Golden Barque* until it went into the gloom. She stayed there for some time, thinking long in the great silence of the bog.

When at last she rose, the canal was clear and cold beneath her. She looked into it. A pale new moon was shining down in the water.

Mary often stood at the door of the cabin on the headland watching the boats that crawled like black snails over the narrow streak of water through the bog. But they were not all like black snails now. There was a Golden Barque among them. Whenever she saw it she smiled, her eyes on the figure that stood by the shaft of the tiller.

One evening she was walking by the canal when *The Golden Barque* passed. The light was very clear and searching. It showed every plank, battered and tar-stained, on the rough hulk, but for all that it lost none of its magic for Mary. The little shrunken driver, head down, the lips moving, walked beside the horse. She heard his low mutters as he passed. The red-faced man was stooping over the side of the boat, swinging out a vessel tied to a rope, to haul up some water. He was singing a ballad in a monotonous voice. A tall, dark, spare man was standing by the funnel, looking vacantly ahead. Then Mary's eyes travelled to the tiller.

Mary stepped back with some embarrassment when she saw the face. She backed into a hawthorn that grew all alone on the canal bank. It was covered with bloom. A shower of the white petals fell about her when she stirred the branches. They clung about her hair like a wreath. He raised his cap and smiled. Mary did not know the face was so eager, so boyish. She smiled a little nervously at last. His face lit up, and he touched his cap again.

The red-faced man stood by the open hatchway going into the hold, the vessel of water in his hand. He looked at Mary and then at the figure beside the tiller.

'Eh, Michael?' the red-faced man said quizzically. The youth turned back to the boat, and Mary felt the blush spreading over her face.

'Michael!'

Mary repeated the name a little softly to herself. The gods had delivered up one of their great secrets.

She watched *The Golden Barque* until the two square slits in the stern that served as port holes looked like two little Japanese eyes. Then she heard a horn blowing. It was the horn they blew to apprise lock-keepers of the approach of a boat. But the nearest lock was a mile off. Besides, it was a long, low sound the horn made, not the short, sharp, commanding blast they blew for lock-keepers. Mary listened to the low sound of the horn, smiling to herself. Afterwards the horn always blew like that whenever *The Golden Barque* was passing the solitary hawthorn.

Mary thought it was very wonderful that *The Golden Barque* should be in the lock one day that she was travelling with her basket to the market in the distant village. She stood a little hesitantly by the lock. Michael looked at her, a welcome in his eyes.

'Going to Bohermeen?' the red-faced man asked.

'Aye, to Bohermeen,' Mary answered.

'We could take you to the next lock,' he said, 'it will shorten the journey. Step in.'

Mary hesitated, as he held out a big hand to help her to the boat. He saw the hesitation and turned to Michael.

'Now, Michael,' he said.

Michael came to the side of the boat, and held out his hand. Mary took it and stepped on board. The red-faced man laughed a little. She noticed that the dark man who stood by the crooked funnel never took his eyes from the stretch of water before him. The driver was already urging the horse to his start on the bank. The brute was gathering his strength for the pull, the muscles standing out on his haunches. They glided out of the lock.

It was half a mile from one lock to another. Michael had bidden her stand beside him at the tiller. Once she looked up at him and she thought the face shy but very eager, the most eager face that ever came across the bog from the great world.

Afterwards, whenever Mary had the time, she would make a cross-cut through the bog to the lock. She would step in and make the mile journey with Michael on *The Golden Barque*. Once, when they were journeying together, Michael slipped something into her hand. It was a quaint trinket, and shone like gold.

'From a strange sailor I got it,' Michael said.

Another day that they were on the barque, the blinding sheets of rain that often swept over the bog came upon them. The red-faced man and the dark man went into the hold. Mary looked about her, laughing. But Michael held out his great waterproof for her. She slipped into it and he folded it about her. The rain pelted them, but they stood together, Michael holding the big coat folded about her. She laughed a little nervously.

'You will be wet,' she said.

Michael did not answer. She saw the eager face coming down close to hers. She leaned against him a little and felt the great strength of his arms about her. They went sailing away together in *The Golden Barque* through all the shining seas of the gods.

'Michael,' Mary said once, 'is it not lovely?'

'The wide ocean is lovely,' Michael said. 'I always think of the wide ocean going over the bog.'

'The wide ocean!' Mary said with awe. She had never seen the wide ocean. Then the rain passed. When the two men came up out of the hold Mary and Michael were standing together by the tiller.

Mary did not go down to the lock after that for some time. She was working in the reclaimed ground on the headland. Once the horn blew late in the night. It blew for a long time, very softly and lowly. Mary sat up in bed listening to it, her lips parted, the memory of Michael on *The Golden Barque* before her. She heard the sound dying away in the distance. Then she lay back on her pillow, saying she would go down to him when *The Golden Barque* was on the return journey.

The figure that stood by the tiller on the return was not Michael's. When Mary came to the lock the red-faced man was telling out the rope, and where Michael always stood by the tiller there was the short strange figure of a man with a pinched, pock-marked face.

When the red-faced man wound the rope round the stump at the lock, bringing the boat to a stand-still, he turned to Mary.

'Michael is gone voyaging,' he said.

'Gone voyaging?' Mary repeated.

'Aye,' the man answered. 'He would be always talking to the foreign sailors in the dock where the canal ends. His eyes would be upon the big masts of the ships. I always said he would go.'

Mary stood there while *The Golden Barque* was in the lock. It looked like a toy ship packed in a wooden box.

'A three-master he went in,' the red-faced man said, as they made ready for the start. 'I saw her standing out for the sea last night. Michael is under the spread of big canvas. He had the blood in him for the wide ocean, the wild blood of the rover.' And the red-faced man, who was the Boss of the boat, let his eyes wander up the narrow neck of water before him.

Mary watched *The Golden Barque* moving away, the grotesque figure standing by the tiller. She stayed there until a pale moon was shining below her, turning over a little trinket in her fingers. At last she dropped it into the water.

It made a little splash, and the vision of the crescent was broken.

Hike and Calcutta

THE BOSS of the boat was standing over the little black stove pouring the drink into enamel cups. His face glowed in the light of the fire. The man with the pock-marked face was squatted Oriental-fashion on the floor. With his face to the lighted candle the man with the tremendously dark countenance was leaning against the water-keg in the corner. His skin was like leather and he never washed. They called him Calcutta because it had been said that a man with a face like his could only come out of the Black Hole of Calcutta. As he leaned against the keg his smouldering eyes were levelled on Hike, the driver.

Hike was at the end of the cabin, fumbling at the bunk. He was muttering to himself. The candle did not throw much light on his stunted figure as he stooped over the bunk.

'Hike,' the Boss said, 'you only drank one fill. Have another.'

Hike did not answer, or even turn round. Hike was deaf.

'Hike!' the Boss cried.

Hike only muttered to himself.

Calcutta stooped over the grate, picked up a piece of coal and took aim. It caught Hike on the head. He turned round, his eyes shining in the semi-gloom like the eyes of a cat.

The Boss laughed a little.

'Drink!' he said. He held out the cup. Hike made no move. Calcutta reached out for the cup and took it to Hike.

Hike shook his head.

A hand shot back and forth suddenly, and Hike got the fluid in the face. It flowed down his cheeks, drops running from his chin and nose with a quick little patter to the floor.

Calcutta turned away from him, laughing. Then the Boss and the man with the pock-marked face seconded the laugh. Hike spluttered and took a step forward, raising a threatening, feeble arm. A scowl most terrible crept into the expression of Calcutta's face as he saw the threat. Hike caught the look and the feeble arm fell. He went over to the bunk and wiped his face in the blanket, then folded it under his arm and went up the little step-ladder through the opening on the deck.

The sky was alive with stars. The canal was still and cool, the country about silent and frozen. He went over to the plank that served as gangway to the bank. It looked like a streak of silver ribbon with a crust of small jewels sparkling upon it. Hike stepped on it nervously and walked down for the bank.

'By God! He's tumbled in,' the Boss swore when he heard the stifled cry and the splash in the water. He ran up the steps, the pock-marked man after him. Calcutta followed leisurely, whistling softly to himself.

Hike was pulling his shrunken body up on the bank when the Boss reached out a helping hand to him. When he stood up Hike was trembling all over, the shining water running down from his clothes. He still held the blanket.

'He's very wet,' the pock-marked man said, 'and it is freezing.'

'Come back to the boat,' the Boss urged.

Hike, holding his arms out stiffly, stood shivering and miserable in two little pools of water gathering about his feet. He looked up at the boat. The figure of Calcutta loomed on the deck, looking down silently on them. Hike hesitated.

'Hike!' Calcutta shouted suddenly. He shouted the nickname in a derisive voice.

Hike turned away and walked down the road, the clothes

and boots soaking and slopping about him at every step. He left a little streak of water in his wake.

'He's gone to the stable,' said the Boss.

'Aye,' Calcutta agreed, 'he'll lie down in the stable.'

The boat started on its journey in the morning as the day was breaking. Hike came up in the dim light, leading the horse from the stable, the whip under his arm. The rope was hooked to the boat, and the men heard Hike urging the horse to the start.

'Gee-up, gee-up!' they heard him cry. The hoofs of the horse struck into the hard ground, and the boat began to move slowly. They had a long journey before them. Hike held aloof from the boatmen at meal times. They heard him coughing and barking all day as he stepped on the bank with the horse. A few times the cough became so violent that he missed the pace and the horse turned his head to him. Hike had to put out his hand and seek support from the rein, catching it near the bit. The horse inclined his head, giving sanction to the support. When they changed horses Hike felt no loss in sympathy; all the horses along the route were accustomed to the touch of his hand.

'He has the rotten old cough back again,' the Boss said, as he stood on the boat.

Calcutta leaned by the funnel, looking at Hike, whistling softly whenever he saw the little man doubled up with the cough. When Hike had to stop dead once, the horse stopped too, neighing. Then Calcutta's voice sang out from the boat, half in derision, half in command:

'Gee-up!' he shouted.

At the word the horse stepped forward with straining steps until he felt the pull of the rope. With the same instinct Hike staggered after him. He kept a hold of the rein the rest of the journey, his hand so close to the mouth of the brute that it was covered with froth.

When the day's journey was ended Hike walked away with the horse to the stable.

'He's going to doss in the stable again,' the Boss said, and

Calcutta's face relaxed, showing a gleam of his teeth.

When the day broke there was no sign of Hike. The Boss went down and called out his name near the stable.

There was no response. He went over to the stable and pushed open the door. A breath of hot, foul air met him. He could not see very well. He could only discern the outline of the wooden partition that divided the stable, and trace the rails of the manger against the wall. The horse stirred his iron-shod hoofs on the cobbles. He saw the animal standing to one side.

'Hike!' the Boss cried.

The horse stirred again, turned his head, and neighed a little. The Boss saw the two little puffs of his breath coming out like steam to the light from the shadows where he stood. He stepped over, and laid a hand on the animal's back. The brute was trembling.

The Boss saw the short, stunted figure huddled on the bed of half-rotted straw at his feet. He stooped down and caught a glimpse of Hike's face. It looked white and prominent, a ghastly visage, in the semi-gloom. He had put out a hand to feel it when a thought struck him.

What if Hike were dead?

He drew back suddenly. The strange silence in the stable was ominous. The place had an atmosphere of sordid tragedy.

What made the brute tremble? Suspicion became a certainty. He walked back to the boat.

'Hike is lying in the stable,' he said. 'There is no stir in him. I think he is dead.'

The pock-marked man raised his cap, and made the sign of the Cross. Calcutta gave a snort of contempt.

'I think he had no friends,' the Boss said at last. He spoke of Hike in the past tense.

'No, he had no friends. How could he?' Calcutta said. Something in his tone made the other look up. The dull eyes were straight ahead on the canal. The Boss, in a vague way, thought he caught some revelation in the dark face. He saw in it an implacable hatred — the sort of hatred that haunts a broken life.

'What do you know of Hike?' he demanded.

'Nothing,' the other replied shortly.

'Go for a priest and doctor. Make a report at the police barrack,' the Boss said to the pock-marked man.

'I will.' The man went down to the cabin to put on his coat.

The Boss walked down the deck, leaning against the tiller at the stern, looking into the yellow water. He gave himself up to one of those meditations that come to people when they are suddenly faced with death, the mysterious death that comes with stealthy steps. The Boss shuddered a little as he remembered the ghastly face of Hike in the dark stable. Then he began to ponder on the strangeness of life and the penalty of death it carried. He got no nearer to the heart of the mystery than the philosophers of the ages.

After a little time he was conscious that Calcutta was standing beside him. The conversation that followed was conducted in lowered voices.

'Do you know what, Boss?'

'What?'

'I was married once.'

'Indeed?'

'I was. The woman came to me in a roundabout kind of way. She was promised to another. She left him for me. I don't know much about the man. She did not speak often of him.'

'That would be natural. She wanted to forget.'

'The thing that came easiest to her was to forget. She forgot that man, and the day came when she forgot me.'

'That was strange.'

'It was. She forgot me because she left me. She went from me to another.'

The Boss had an idea that all this was irrelevant, but that it at least threw some light on the ugly, brooding manner of Calcutta.

'I'm sorry for you,' said the Boss awkwardly.

The other laughed, a short hard laugh. 'Oh, I did not mind,' he said. 'It was no great concern to me when she left.'

'No?'

'What I felt was, she left me for a man that I had a hatred for. She left me for a man that made me feel so little. The man she went to was Hike.'

'So that is why you have been down on Hike?'

'I hounded him all right. I came on this boat to hound him. He knew it. I only stayed on the boat because I wanted to see him dying on the bank, coughing up his inside. I was never so happy as I was yesterday when the spasms were smashing him up. He knew all that very well, and I think it helped to kill him. It was that woman who made me hate him above all living things.'

'And what became of the woman? Where is she now?'

'Where is she?' the other repeated, his eyes following up the narrow neck of water. 'How do I know. But I hope she's in hell.'

He walked back to his accustomed place by the funnel.

The pock-marked man raised a cry from the bank. His hand was pointing down the road. The Boss followed its direction. He gave a muttered cry. Walking up from the stable, leading his horse, was Hike.

He raised his head as he came to the boat. His colour was sickly, his eyes pathetic. But the Boss thought he saw a dumb doggedness, a smouldering defiance, in the expression as the eyes wandered to the figure of the dark man standing by the funnel.

'I overslept myself,' said Hike. 'I had a little headache.'

The boat moved on after a time. Hike did not cough so much that day. The sun was shining pleasantly from the sky; there was warmth in the air. The scowl in the face of the man by the blackened funnel was deeper.

The Boss had a few words with Hike when opportunity offered. He had a difficulty in thinking of the half-hunched, miserable person that stood before him as figuring in such an affair as Calcutta had mentioned. But then, he reflected, who has ever been able to account for the ways of men?

'Hike,' he said, in his blunt manner, 'were you ever married?'

Hike raised the pathetic, large eyes that often go with half-deformed people. A sentimental look came into them, heightening their strangeness.

'I was — and I was not,' Hike said, then coughed.

His gaze wandered to *The Golden Barque* and the sinister figure that stood beside the funnel. 'There was one that was everything to me that a wife should be,' Hike confided, the note of sentimentality more pronounced.

'Now, that was very nice,' the Boss said, for he knew he could venture some mild humour where there was so much emotion.

Hike's eyes grew humid. 'She was an angel,' he said, a catch in his voice.

The Boss, who was healthy-minded, controlled his florid features.

'Where is she now?' he asked, half casually.

Hike hesitated. He had to bring his mind back from a riot of sentiment. He had to dispose of something in his throat.

'She went,' he admitted at last, half enigmatically. Then he added, 'I hope she is in heaven.'

The Boss walked back to the boat. The thing that was a while ago a very tragic business had begun to show the underlap of comedy. When he found himself near Calcutta he said, still casually, 'I know where that wife of yours is now.'

'I don't want to be told,' the other answered. 'My hope is that she's in hell.'

'Well, she's not. She's in heaven.'

Calcutta laughed hoarsely.

'I might have guesed it,' he said.

'Guessed what?'

'That the devil himself could not hold her when he got her.'

The Boss walked down the deck. He gazed upon the sun that was growing low in the sky. Some great trees were standing out stark on the landscape. When he turned back again he saw Hike stepping beside the horse on the bank, something in his half humps that was stubborn, distorted, grotesque. Calcutta was by the funnel, his eyes smouldering, unblinking, implacable, as they followed the steps of the driver beside the horse. He was the sleuth hound of the strange, silent hunt.

The Boss pondered on the ways of men, and again there was no explanation, no solution of the problem. The underlap of comedy was gone. In the rose light of the falling day the sense of human tragedy dragged out on the stretch of yellow water was uppermost to his mind.

He shrugged his shoulders as he put out his hand for the shaft of the tiller.

Nan Hogan's House

WHEN MRS. PAUL MANTON lifted the latch and pushed open the door of Nan Hogan's house she was rooted to the spot by the sight which presented itself to her view.

Nan Hogan was propped up by the side of the hearth in a weird collection of old clothes, or, as Mrs. Manton called them, 'old brillauns' gathered together 'in long ages and generations'. But Nan Hogan's uncompromising head and shoulders rose out of the pillows, and her one fearless steel-grey eye took Mrs. Paul Manton in with steady and frank displeasure.

'The Lord save us; what came over you, Nan Hogan?' Mrs. Manton asked.

'The weakness came over me,' Nan Hogan made answer in her traditional note of discontent.

'And there isn't a spark of fire in the place,' Mrs. Manton declared, moving down to the hearth.

'What does that signify,' Nan Hogan said. 'People ought to be thankful to have a spark of life in their bodies, and they maybe with neighbours that don't care the toss of a button whether they're dead or living.'

Nan gathered some of the clothes up about her as she spoke. Mrs. Manton made no reply. She brought an armful of turf from a box in a corner, and built up a fire on the hearth.

'When were you taken bad?' she asked as she fanned the flames with her apron.

'Last night, ma'am,' Nan replied, coldly. 'If it might

concern you to know the exact hour I'm sorry I can't strengthen your knowledge.'

'Is it the rheumatism?' Mrs. Manton went on, ignoring Nan's tone.

'No, ma'am, it isn't no rheumatism, for that's always in the four bones of me.'

Mrs. Manton gave some hot milk to the patient.

'I thought it was a nice place,' Nan Hogan said, sipping the milk, 'where a woman was left to die on the floor with nothing more Christian near her than a drowsy cat.' And Nan made a feeble movement with one of her feet in the heap of clothes to throw off a sleepy cat ensconced in the arm of an old jacket. The cat only rolled over softly, and curled himself into the remains of a once glorious mantilla.

'Couldn't you make a noise, or call out or do something?' Mrs. Manton suggested.

'I could indeed, pet,' Nan replied, sarcastically, 'if I had the strength for it. But what is a body to do when the weakness is upon her? There I was, going over them articles of clothes, contriving to see what sort of a skirt I might be making out of them, when, lo and behold, the power went out of my limbs. I just lay back, ma'am, where I am, and pulled the clothes the best way I could about me, to keep from perishing.'

'I'll be making the bed for you,' Mrs. Manton said, going into the little room.

'It's case equal where a body is left to rot,' Nan went on in the same monotonous, metallic voice which had long ago lost all its provoking rasp for Mrs. Paul Manton. 'But I was thinking to myself that Kilbeg would cut a handsome figure when it was published to the world that it let an oul' creature die without the comfort of priest or the charity of doctor.'

Mrs. Manton in the room inside began to rattle the furniture and make a noise. It was her way for resenting Nan Hogan's tone. Nan perked her head when she heard the racket in the room, and her voice rose higher and shriller. 'And more betoken,' she cried, 'there's them in Kilbeg that wouldn't ask better than hearing of a sudden death. There's one cabin-hunter in Kilbeg that'd go down on her bare marrow-bones to give thanks that I died with the company of a cat by the black hearth.'

For some reason a chair got knocked over at this moment in the room, and Nan Hogan lay back a little, a certain expression of ugly satisfaction in her face. Presently Mrs. Manton came out and did some tidying-up about the kitchen. Then she removed the bundle of rags from around Nan Hogan, stowing them away in the big bin that stood over against the wall. But when it came to helping Nan Hogan to bed Mrs. Paul Manton's natural vigour gave way. The woman was so helpless that she could not put a leg under her.

'Didn't I tell you I was crippled?' Nan demanded. 'I suppose, ma'am, you take me for a liar and an imposter, and the grave opening up in front of me?'

'The cramps are in your legs, Nan Hogan,' Mrs. Manton said, 'and no wonder. I'll be going out for Mrs. Denny Hynes.'

And while Mrs. Manton was away for help Nan Hogan sat dismantled on her floor, her one eye looking out of the little window with that eternal and unblinking pessimism which gave her such a sinister appearance. Mrs. Paul Manton and Mrs. Denny Hynes helped Nan Hogan into her bed as gently as they could.

'I'm beholden to you,' Nan said with dry scepticism. 'But it's not long I'll be troubling the people of Kilbeg.'

'Tim O'Halloran will be over to-morrow,' Mrs. Manton said. 'He'll be coming with the relief. And maybe he could send you a doctor.'

'It's great good that will be to me, indeed,' Nan said with a little hard laugh. 'You might as well be telling me that Kilbeg will be giving me the compliment of a big funeral when it gets shut of me.'

The women had to listen to a good deal of the same kind of criticism of Kilbeg for the rest of the day.

When the news of Nan Hogan's sudden weakness spread through Kilbeg any of the people who could at all spare a little time 'took a chase down to see what way the creature was'.

Accordingly, for the rest of the day, there was a continual movement of visitors over the little stile and down the strip of road leading into Nan Hogan's house.

Her house stood right at the bottom of the village, pushed in, so to speak, from the irregular line of cabins and with its back turned upon them all. Kilbeg in its construction had never come under the tyranny of the architect or the conventionality of the engineer. There was no designing, no mapping and planning, no consideration of aspect, and no surveying of the site. The houses were put up by the people according as they were wanted, and under conditions of the most perfect individual liberty. One cabin, so to speak, did not care a snap for the other, and showed it. If you were a sociable person, for instance, you hooked your habitation on to a number of others. If you were of a retiring disposition you planted yourself away in from the road or went down into a dip in the ground. If you were aggressive or overbearing you put your house on a commanding view, and if you were nasty and wanted to be disagreeable you built your cabin in front of your enemy's door, so that he would have to walk about your house to get in or out of his own, and the movements of his family would be under your constant observation. The cabins of Kilbeg were pitched according to the temperaments of the inhabitants, so that you could almost tell by looking at them what manner of mortal sheltered under each roof. Nan Hogan's house gave expression to Nan's opinion of Kilbeg, for no matter what other cabin door you stood at, Nan's house had an angle pointing at you.

Nan Hogan sat propped up on her bed all day receiving her visitors. She measured every fresh arrival with her solitary eye. Her tongue never faltered in its grim humour. Every word of caustic greeting held its sting. The sour expression never faded from the features as the hours passed, nor the tone of discontent from her voice. But I doubt much if Cleopatra in all her glory ever relished a parade of obsequious beauties kowtowing before her throne as much as Nan Hogan relished her levee in Kilbeg that day. There was only one cloud on the brilliancy of her reception — Sara Finnessy never turned up. The very sight of Sara Finnessy stirred up every inch of venom in Nan Hogan. For Sara Finnessy to cross her threshold, while she enjoyed all the advantage of her sudden weakness, would spell a very ecstasy to the patient.

The bitterness between Nan Hogan and Sara Finnessy was very real and of long standing. It went back to the day that Nan found herself utterly alone and deserted in her cabin. The last of her family, the boy upon whom all her affections were lavished, had gone away from her that day. With him had disappeared the eldest boy of Sara Finnessy, 'a rascal who left Kilbeg that he might cheat and swindle the wide world', Nan Hogan had said. These two youthful adventurers of Kilbeg had joined a band of wanderers who were taking flight from the hills about Ballinaiske 'to sail the waters of all the oceans in their sailoring'. Nan Hogan believed, as she believed in her God, that it was young Finnessy who had lured her boy from his home, and all her bitterness was heaped upon the head of Sara Finnessy from that day to this.

The people had pity for Nan Hogan. She had never what they called 'the even temper or the mannerly way,' but most of them knew her when she was a proud woman with her family about her. God had taken her man from Nan Hogan, leaving her with a young family of two daughters and two boys. She had striven to bring up her little family. The eldest girl went in the decline just as she was gathering the shape of a woman. The second girl married a boy over from Boherlahan, and they emigrated to America. They were understood to be striving the best way they could in the Republic down to this day. The second boy wasted away after his sister, and the night he was waked Nan Hogan sat by his bed telling the people that poor Thomaseen had never any heart for the rough world.

It was a poor story enough, the story of Nan Hogan. It can be understood how her heart wound itself about the only one left her of the flock, the eldest boy, an active, strong, big-hearted, giddy-headed, impulsive youth. It cannot be so easily understood how Nan Hogan felt when one day that boy left her alone in her house and in the world. It was little wonder she had the pity of Kilbeg. She had seen all her care scattered to the far places of the world, or drawn to the grave, and if she strove on after that, keeping her cabin together, putting in her day's work in the fields and contriving to sustain her independence, it was, as her neighbours said, because she had the courage of her own heart.

It was not unnatural, therefore, if Nan Hogan became soured against the world — that is to say, Kilbeg. The one privilege left her was the right to complain, and she took advantage of it to the full. The neighbours bore with her as well as their humanity allowed them; they tried to remember her sorrow, and left her the comfort of her tongue — all except Sara Finnessy, whose peculiar psychological construction allowed her to give Nan Hogan no great latitude. 'A ranting old hare,' Sara Finnessy called Nan Hogan, but Sara Finnessy's toleration extended so far that she kept out of Nan's way as far as the geographical disposition of Kilbeg would permit.

However, if Nan Hogan was denied the comfort of an attack on Sara Finnessy, while she had the advantage of her sudden weakness, it was some sort of consolation to her to see Christy Finnessy crossing her threshold in the cool of the evening. Christy came in heavily to the house, and fully conscious that he bore, in the judgment of the patient, the burden of his woman's sins. The eye of Nan Hogan kindled when she heard the step of Christy Finnessy upon her floor.

'I hear 'tis how you were taken bad sudden,' Christy said in his stupid way, stooping rather unnecessarily as he entered the doorway of the little room. Nan looked at him with her searching eye, her mouth drawn tight and hard. Christy thought, with a little pang of relief, that maybe Nan's speech was taken from her in the attack. The thought was short-lived.

'I suppose,' said Nan, 'that you were sent down to take the dimensions of me coffin?'

'Well, no, Nan, I was not,' Christy put in mildly.

'You're a great man,' Nan said in her level voice, 'a great man, Christy Finnessy, and I always said it. I never thought of you yet but that I remembered the saying that God makes the back for the burden.'

Christy moved down to the end of the room where Nan held him in her eye. 'God is good,' Christy said, with a feeling of light-heartedness.

'The courage that always stood to you,' Nan said, 'the courage and the strength of your back. You may well thank God for giving you both, or it's long long ago Sara Finnessy would be in the company of Mrs. Lowry and myself — two widow-women with mourning in our hearts.'

'Mrs. Lowry had wisdom,' Christy managed to put in. 'She never gave herself over to the grief like you did, Nan Hogan.'

Nan Hogan hitched herself on her pillow with an air of roused interest that made Christy Finnessy's heart sink.

'The more I ponder over your case, Christy,' Nan said, 'the more respect I have for your strength. "If he was another," I'd say to myself, "she'd have him stretched long ago the day." And sure the harmless poor men of the hills ought never be done giving their praise to you. What one of them knew but that it might be himself would fall into Sara's hands when she was roving the country on the lookout? But like the brave heart you had, my son, you took away the danger the day she led you up to the marriage rails.'

'Well,' said Christy, bridling, 'I never had any regrets over that same day.'

'That's it, honey,' said Nan, 'you bore up, all your life

with the courage of ten men. No one ever yet heard the poor word of complaint on your lips, only you to be striving over the road like a mule that'd be put to the pull of a great caravan. You were never without the admiration of the people.'

It was with great relief Christy Finnessy saw the Widow Lowry bustling into the little room. The Widow settled the pillows about Nan, and laid critical fingers on her forehead.

'You're fine and natural, thank God,' the Widow Lowry said. 'It was only just a passing fit.'

'What odds does it make?' Nan said. 'And indeed you oughtn't to be giving such sad word for Christy Finnessy to be bringing back home with him. It's little welcome there'll be before him if he hasn't the story to tell that Nan Hogan is drawing on her last gasp.'

'Christy Finnessy has no wish to carry the black word,' the Widow said, and Christy looked his thanks to the Widow.

'Christy's wish indeed!' Nan exclaimed. 'When was Christy's wish of any account in the house of Sara Finnessy? Isn't it only now I was telling him of the respect and admiration he had of the world. No one ought to know that better than yourself, ma'am, you a woman that put a couple of men through your own hands.'

The Widow Lowry laughed good-humouredly. 'I'll do for a few more of them yet,' she said.

'Then if that be your way,' said Nan Hogan, 'you're the fortunate woman you didn't strike on Christy Finnessy. When Sara didn't as much as sour the man's temper, sure he'd be like a fiery young colt to-day if he fell into your own hands.'

Christy Finnessy moved down to the door.

'I must put a coal in the pipe at the fire,' he said, going out into the kitchen.

Nan's voice followed him out. 'Tell Sara,' she said, 'that she isn't shut of Nan Hogan yet. That funeral she's expecting won't move up the village for another while. And there's no telling who might not be going before her. God be praised. Christy Finnessy, you're the greatest constitution of a man that ever threw a shadow across the floor.'

Nan lay back on her pillows, her eye closing, and her face, the Widow Lowry thought, becoming more pallid.

'You have no right to be over-reaching yourself,' the Widow said, testily.

Nan's eye opened and took in the Widow with some concern. 'I'd be satisfied,' she said, 'if that Christy Finnessy was not such a moosaun. I'm in dread now he won't bring my words up home with him. It's a poor case when a body is stretched with the dint of weakness, maybe to be wasting me words on a man that has no retention for them.'

When Christy Finnessy got home he sat down by the fire.

'Well,' his woman asked expectantly, 'what way is she?'

'She says,' Christy said, 'that she has a weakness.' And he knocked the heel of his pipe of tobacco out on the palm of his hand.

'And has she?' Mrs. Finnessy asked.

'Well,' Christy said, refilling the pipe, 'if she has I'm thinking it must not be in her tongue. She's keeping her intellect clear to the last.'

Mrs. Sara Finnessy leaned over to her man. 'Was she saying anything?' she asked, the battle-light coming into her eyes in anticipation.'

'She was. She was saying many a thing.'

'Giving out about myself, I'll engage,' Sara suggested.

Christy yawned and stretched out his toes to the fire. 'I couldn't rightly say,' he said. 'She was talking in a sort of back-hand way. And whether or which it's all gone from me memory now. It went from me and I coming up the road.' And as Christy could not be got beyond this declaration his woman looked upon him with open contempt.

When the Widow Lowry was coming up home later she saw Sara Finnessy leaning up miserably against the side of the door, her hands folded under her arms.

'She's gone into a kind of a drowse,' the Widow told her.

'Was Christy telling you anything?'

'No, ma'am, he was not,' Mrs. Finnessy replied. 'There's no comfort to be had in him. 'Tisn't the first time in my life that I felt the hardship of a man that has no gift of retention.'

And the Widow Lowry caught the same note of pained regret in the tone of Sara Finnessy as she had detected in the voice of Nan Hogan.

The Widow Lowry laughed a little to herself as she turned in to her home. 'Christy,' she said, 'has taken the good out of the day for both of them. He's the poorest ambassador that stands in the country.'

When Tim O'Halloran, the relieving officer, came to Kilbeg from Boherlahan the next day with the outdoor relief to a few destitute people, he found Nan Hogan in a poor way. She was shrunken up in the bed.

'Leave the few shillings on the dresser, Tim,' she said.

'I must send the doctor to you, Nan,' Tim said. 'You're looking a bit shook.'

'I got a weakness,' Nan explained, 'a great weakness in the legs. It's more through good luck than through any neighbourly grace that you hadn't an ugly case in me this day, Tim O'Halloran. I suppose it wouldn't be any great pleasure to you to find me a corpse upon the floor. But it was nearly coming to that through the charity of Kilbeg.'

'You'd be better off in the hospital,' Tim said. 'You'd get the right care there.'

'Is it sending me into the Poorhouse you have a mind?' Nan asked quickly, some of the old fire coming into her eye.

'It would be the best place for you,' Tim answered, bluntly.

Nan Hogan looked steadily and suspiciously at him for a minute. 'Tim O'Halloran,' she demanded, 'has any person in Kilbeg put you up to send me to the Poorhouse?'

'I wouldn't like to rob Kilbeg of its store of wisdom,' Tim answered. 'I'm coming to it long enough, and I never expected any great enlightenment from its people. They never disappointed me.'

This reply was much to Nan's heart.

'It would be like a shaft of light shining down from heaven to Sara Finnessy if she saw me heading for the Poorhouse,' Nan said.

'Well, now,' said Tim, in his most judicial tone, 'maybe if she thought that the good treatment would put you on your legs again it would put a cloud over the light.'

Nan remained thinking over this view very quietly for some time.

'And, indeed, Nan,' Tim urged, 'you're no great envy to anyone as long as you're stretched there the way you are. It might be a great satisfaction to Sara Finnessy to say that Nan Hogan was now no more than Denny Hynes, a bed-ridden man.'

And Tim left Nan Hogan to ponder over his words while he went out to deliver some instructions to the neighbours. Tim advised the neighbours that it was well to hammer it into the head of Nan Hogan that it was the great wish of Sara Finnessy's heart to see her lying helpless on her bed until the Lord called her.

He had some difficulty in getting the neighbours to play upon the prejudices of the patient. They resented the Poorhouse for any person in Kilbeg. It was only when Tim O'Halloran laid the lie of Nan Hogan at their feet that the Widow Lowry and Mrs. Paul Manton consented to do his bidding.

The news that Nan Hogan was about to be removed in the ambulance to the Poorhouse cast a gloom over Kilbeg. The Workhouse Car, as they called it, was only seen in Kilbeg in years of acute distress. The very thought of it was repugnant to every heart upon the hillsides. Many of the people said they would almost as soon carry out Nan Hogan in her coffin as see her taken away in the Poorhouse Car. It was to them an emblem of death and pestilence and horror, a black vulture that hovered over places where the people lay broken, a thing that had direct descent from the Famine, that carried with it an atmosphere of soup-houses and proselytism, that smelt of a foul traffic in soul-selling and body-snatching, the relic of a tyranny that held the memory of the Penal Laws in the grind of its wheels.

The Widow Lowry and Mrs. Paul Manton went in and out to the sick room that day with an instinctive feeling that public opinion outside was against them in this work. It was only the belief that the end justified the means — that Nan Hogan's recovery depended upon her treatment in the hospital — that kept them to their promise to Tim O'Halloran.

The Widow Lowry was in the kitchen, looking after the preparation of some medicine which had been provided for the patient when Mrs. Manton came out of the room to lend a hand. Mrs. Manton found the Widow Lowry fiddling rather blindly among the delft on the dresser.

'What's delaying you?' Mrs. Manton asked, going up to her. The Widow turned away, groping for the fireplace with a little cry. Mrs. Manton caught a sight of her face.

'Do you think now that this is going to do Nan Hogan any good?' Mrs. Manton demanded severely. The Widow sat down on a stool by the fire.

'I couldn't help thinking of the way this home was scattered,' the Widow said. 'To think of her man, and her children, and the heart she kept up through it all. I had my own troubles, God knows, but what were they to the troubles of Nan Hogan!'

'That's a nice way to be helping the woman, Mrs. Manton said. 'It's a shame for you, a great shame for you.' Mrs. Manton tried to keep up the severity in her voice, but the last word broke in a little gasp. She, like the Widow Lowry, had to grope for the fireplace. They sat down together, two dim figures in the smoke on Nan Hogan's hearth, wiping their eyes in their aprons and crying quietly.

'I was here when the weight of her troubles came upon her one by one, but I never thought it would come to this.'

'Did he say when the Car was to be here?' in a whisper that was full of the pending dread.

'I hadn't the courage to ask him.'

The Poorhouse Car came rumbling up through the village when the shadows were deepening. But it would take more than the charity of the gathering night to cloak the ugliness of the Poorhouse Car. The shaggy, ill-kept, slow-looking brute that drew it seemed conscious of the weight behind him. The driver, in his pauper clothes, sat lop-sided on the seat, the whip dangling from his hands in a spiritless, slipshod fashion. The Car was black and heavy and lurched over the road like a ship that had lost its ballast, a dark, covered-in structure, with a door at the back. The shafts tilted over the shoulders of the horse, as if the harness were a misfit and the horse too small for the vehicle. The people stood silent by the way as it came up, the children running frightened into the houses, for they had heard such evil things of this spectre during the day that it held more terror for them than the Headless Coach.

Mrs. Manton and the Widow Lowry heard the sound of the wheels turning upon the road from a great distance. They bustled about the room, talking a little wildly and making such noise as might kill the sound for Nan Hogan. But Nan, too, had heard the ominous rumble. She spoke no word, but her eye was fixed on the little window of the room waiting for the thing to make a dark shadow across it. It passed at last, a hitched-up patch of black in the dim light. Tim O'Halloran came in with a few of the men, walking softly and speaking in undertones. Mrs. Paul Manton and the Widow Lowry were making Nan ready for the journey, talking to her with forced cheerfulness, when suddenly Mrs. Paul Manton threw up her arms, and stepping out from the door fled from Nan Hogan's house. The Widow Lowry, whose voice had become a little breathless, thought to cover the retreat as well as she could, but Nan was wonderfully alert and susceptible to the things going on about her. A wan smile passed over her face when she saw Mrs. Manton throwing up her arms and clearing. She still held her peace, and was carried out in a dead silence by the men to the waiting vehicle which loomed before the door. The feet of the men shuffled over the ground, and Nan saw the figures of neighbours standing about in the shadows. She had been carried quite close to the door of the ambulance when something seemed to strike her.

'Lock the door of the house,' she called out in her well-known voice. A few people fumbled at the door, found the key, and turned it in the lock.

The Widow Lowry was saying to one of the women, 'Talk of courage and heart! The world never yet saw the like of it!'

'Kilbeg isn't shut of Nan Hogan yet,' Nan's voice sang out from the ambulance door.

Tim O'Halloran was busy seeing to the care of the patient, and the Widow Lowry to singing her praises, or they would have made some effort to prevent the blunder that followed. In the confusion at the door a woman got hold of the key just as Nan called out from the Poorhouse Car — 'Bring me that key, now. I'm not giving it up yet.'

A figure stepped towards the ambulance, and held out the key. The next moment a loud wail broke out upon the air.

It was Sara Finnessy who held out the key to Nan Hogan. Kilbeg never could say whether she did it in malice or in mistaken repentance, for Sara Finnessy herself scorned to make a declaration. But whatever the motive, it had an instantaneous effect on Nan Hogan. She wailed and screamed in the ambulance and the people began to gather excitedly close to the vehicle. Sara Finnessy threw the key, some said in terror, into the ambulance and rushed up the road home. Nan Hogan was seen to be battling with her arms in the ambulance with the woman who had come as a sort of companion from the Poorhouse. She was tearing the wraps from about her and could be seen dimly, like a spectre, fighting her way to the door of the vehicle. Presently she reached it, clinging to the door and swaying about like a wraith making loud complaint and calling on the people to take her back into her home. Tim O'Halloran pleaded with her to go quietly, but Nan battled with the courage of despair.

The people were now drawn close about the Poorhouse Car and Tim O'Halloran could hear hoarse murmurs breaking out among them. Tim O'Halloran knew the people of Kilbeg. He knew that the painful battle Nan Hogan was making was rousing anger in their hearts, and that it only required a lead from one man or one woman to stir them to action and violence. He knew that should one blow be struck Nan Hogan would be forcibly carried back to her house, and the Poorhouse Car wrecked — reduced to matchwood — before her door. It was a moment for decisive action. Tim O'Halloran turned to the crowd. 'Fardy Lalor,' he called out, 'stand here by the step.'

Fardy Lalor moved up to the door of the ambulance, and stood there quietly, his face to the crowd. Tim O'Halloran caught the screaming patient in his arms and carried her bodily into the van. He stepped back, slammed the door, and shouted to the driver to move on.

Kilbeg never witnessed such a distressing sight before. The Poorhouse Car lurched slowly up the village, the muffled screams and protests of Nan Hogan coming from within, Tim O'Halloran and Fardy Lalor walking close to the doorstep like a bodyguard, and an excited crowd of people behind them. It was not until they were a mile out on the Boherlahan road that the wails of Nan Hogan died away within the hideous conveyance. Then the people began to fall back.

Tim O'Halloran wiped the perspiration from his forehead, and heaved a sigh of relief. 'They were within an ace of killing her,' he said. 'Only for yourself, Fardy Lalor, there would be bad work in Kilbeg this night.'

'She'll never do any good after this,' Fardy Lalor answered.

Tim O'Halloran shook his head. 'I know Nan Hogan a great long while,' he said. 'I saw her putting many a storm over her head. You'll see her back in Kilbeg again.'

*   *   *

While Nan Hogan was undergoing treatment in the Boherlahan Union Hospital, she did not surrender her right to give audible expression to her thoughts. Nan's thoughts were not sweetened by her surroundings. But she had no longer a monopoly in gloomy speculation, for her fellow-sufferers in the ward were all more or less inclined to take a morbid view of life. This fact took a great deal of point from Nan's outlook. She had a feeling that she was only throwing ink on a black sky. There was no satisfaction in holding parleys with patients who paid back gloom for gloom. She missed the lively background of Kilbeg, the conflict of outlook that brought out the light and shade of her battling will.

Instinctively, Nan Hogan turned her attention to one Maura Casey, a sprightly little woman, who had been promoted from the able-bodied ward of the Poorhouse to the position of helper in the hospital. Maura Casey was a sort of understrapper to the nurses described, I believe, in official documents as a wards-maid. The nurses and doctor had, in Nan Hogan's view, become so much a part of the ritual of the hospital that she got little satisfaction in their company. They kept the machinery of the place in smooth motion, were sort of skilled engineers, who oiled the ailments of the day and greased the pains of the night. They kept the life in you up to the last possible moment, and when they could keep it in you no longer, they passed you out for disposal by another department. But Maura Casey, Nan Hogan felt, was nearer to the humanities; the only person who seemed to be out of gear in the place, whose movements and manners were not regulated by invisible machinery. Maura came in the door carrying some breath of the irresponsible world outside about her. To Maura Casey, therefore, Nan turned for fleeting moments of companionship. The fact that Maura Casey could only lend her ear to Nan Hogan whenever the eyes of the authorities were off guard, sweetened the acquaintanceship.

Maura Casey was not for some time very responsive, for she was some five years 'looking at cases' in that place. Her interest in earthly woes had in that time and in the peculiar circumstances, got somewhat blunted. It was the talk of Nan Hogan about her house and the constancy of a dream which haunted her sleeping hours, that aroused the interest of Maura Casey. Nan would tell Maura Casey about her house and her dream while Maura scrubbed the floor about her bed.

Nan Hogan's description of her house would sound fantastic to anybody who knew Kilbeg, but when one is reduced to fiddling on the one string the temptation to introduce variations, with, perhaps, some flighty passages, some thrills and shivers, proves too strong for the artistic temperament. Maura Casey got it into her head that Nan Hogan, under stress of a sudden weakness in the legs, had to leave a splendid dwelling in the village of Kilbeg to the mercy of a most unworthy cat. The effect of this picture of the abandoned mansion in Kilbeg was heightened by the dream of Nan Hogan, faithfully recorded to Maura Casey the morning following its persistent recurrence. It was under cover of this remarkable dream that Nan Hogan introduced, with lawful embellishments, the villain of the piece, Sara Finnessy. Sara Finnessy was described with great relish by Nan Hogan, so much relish that Maura Casey would kneel back on her heels on the floor until the lather of disinfecting soap evaporated from her scrubbing brush. Maura Casey felt that the gallows had been cheated of at least one female monster. She could see this woman fiend dancing a strange, triumphant dance about a closed up, silent house, throwing a sort of Highland fling at the front door, capering, round the gables in a crazy reel, and bringing the performance to a close with an ecstatic, standing jump on to the roof. Maura Casey had no imagination, but this picture was put magically before her by Nan Hogan in her descriptions of her nightly vision.

The thing grew so much on Maura Casey that one day, when she had got a few hours' leave of absence from Boherlahan Hospital she was seized with such an overpowering curiosity that she footed it over to Kilbeg to view the deserted mansion of Nan Hogan, and, if possible, and at a safe distance, steal a look at the thrilling Sara Finnessy.

Maura Casey saw both wonders in Kilbeg, and came back with a droop in the corners of her mouth. When Nan Hogan continued her recitals afterwards Maura Casey paid less heed to her words, and more to her scrubbing brushes. 'Raving the woman is,' Maura Casey told herself, 'raving for death.'

But the empty cabin in Kilbeg had an unexpected psychological effect on Maura Casey. It was such a cabin as she had often ambitioned. She had been a woman who knocked about from one workhouse to another, tramping over the roads, before she settled down in Boherlahan, and earned her promotion to the hospital. Like many other homeless creatures, Maura Casey lacked the love of wandering that is of the gipsy and tinker blood. She was a wanderer through necessity, and not from choice. Maura Casey had always held an opinion that she was a born housekeeper, and that it was one of the ironies of life, the caprices of Fate, that she should never be able to claim a little house of her own. She liked to hang about small cabins for that reason, fancying to herself what she could be doing had she the ownership of one. For the same reason she liked rather lonely, out-of-the-way, quiet places, her instinct telling her that if she ever could lay claim to a cabin of her own her best chance lay in such places.

Maura Casey, with the home hunger in her heart, had faced the winds and the unending journeys for many years, until a bad winter came with a heavy fall of snow. She had been caught on the hills in the midst of it, and had suffered so much from exposure that she sought the sanctuary of Boherlahan Union and stayed there ever since. Her ambition to become a housekeeper and a householder was nipped, and lay dormant until she saw Nan Hogan's empty house in Kilbeg, after which she got into the habit of long spells of silent reflection in the intervals of her labour in the hospital.

Soon after Nan Hogan missed Maura Casey from the hospital. She was told that Maura had given up the job — 'taken her discharge,' as they put it — and had gone out again into the world. Nan Hogan became low-spirited as a result, even though they were, as she said, 'coaxing back a little life to her limbs.'

In the meantime, Kilbeg had settled down to its normal condition, and the agitation created by the distressing departure from Kilbeg had subsided to various speculations as to whether Nan was ever likely to return to her home.

One fine morning, however, Kilbeg was astonished to see smoke coming out of the chimney of Nan Hogan's house. It went up into the blue air with a sort of flourish, proclaiming to the world that life was once more active under the roof. The wild word went about that Nan Hogan had mysteriously returned in the dead of the night. The people who were earliest astir tumbled over each other across the little stile and down the little pathway to give her welcome. The front door was locked against them, and there was no response to a few impatient thumps upon it. The Widow Lowry was the first to make her way in by the backyard. She found the back door wide open.

A strange woman was sitting by the hearth, enjoying a cup of tea with an air of great contentment. She looked very much at home, and quite unmoved by the astounded appearance of the Widow.

'Who — who are you?' the Widow asked at last, as the rest of the people grouped themselves about her.

'Me? — Oh, I'm Maura Casey.'

'Maura Casey?'

'The same, ma'am. Maura Casey, over from Boherlahan.'

'What is she doing here?' Paul Manton asked of his neighbours.

'House-keeping,' Maura Casey made answer.

There was a little embarrassed silence, during which Maura Casey went on enjoying her early cup of tea.

'And where is Nan Hogan?' Mrs. Manton demanded.

'She's in the hospital, talking by day and raving by night.'

'Raving by night?'

'Aye, she's raving for death.'

'And how do you know?'

'Why shouldn't I know? Was I in the Boherlahan Hospital for nothing?'

'Was it Nan sent you to the house?'

Maura Casey laid down her cup and saucer, and wiped her mouth with her apron with a gesture that proclaimed her satisfaction with the tea. Then she walked over collectedly to the door, standing up close to Mrs. Paul Manton.

'I'm thinking, ma'am,' Maura Casey said, 'that Kilbeg was never noted for the manners of its people.'

The people drew back a little from Maura Casey. She carried about her the air of a woman who knew her business and was sure of her authority.

'It's rather soon to be talking of manners,' Mrs. Manton said, with some show of doubt. 'Was it Nan Hogan gave you the rights of her house?'

'That, ma'am, makes no matter at all to you. When I ask the rights of your house, if you have one, it'll be time enough for you to show the height of your breeding.'

'The law will settle it all,' Paul Manton said, walking slowly away, most of the people following him in silence. Mrs. Paul Manton and the Widow Lowry lingered behind.

'Did you say,' the Widow asked in a more conciliatory tone, 'that poor Nan Hogan is raving for death?'

'That she is. And if you are a friend of Sara Finnessy you'd best be telling her not to go next or near Nan Hogan while she lasts.'

This revelation of inside information into the state of Nan Hogan's mind on the part of the newcomer had a very convincing effect on the Kilbeg women. They were ready to back down and continue the interview with Maura Casey, in the hope of gathering more insight into her person and history.

'Is it how she sent you to keep the house aired and warm for her, thinking she'd be coming back soon?' Mrs. Manton asked, with some show of acknowledging Maura Casey's authority.

'It is no wish of Nan Hogan,' Maura Casey replied, 'that her mind should be made known to any person in this place.'

And Maura Casey, with an active movement, tucked up her skirt over her petticoat and dashed into her household activities. The Widow Lowry and Mrs. Paul Manton took the hint and departed.

People hung about the house all day. Every movement of the new arrival was noted and duly commented upon. Maura Casey, it was conceded, was a woman of wonderful energy. Already Nan Hogan's house was beginning to brighten and take on a fresh, cared-for appearance.

'I tell you what,' a man said, 'Nan Hogan knew what she was doing when she sent the like of that woman into her house.'

Sara Finnessy was expected to show some sort of welcome to the newcomer. It struck people that a substitute — any sort of a substitute — for Nan Hogan would be satisfactory to Mrs. Finnessy. Sara Finnessy was moody, however, and reserved her judgment on the unexpected development until the close of the day. Then she broke out.

'She's an imposter,' Sara Finnessy declared. 'She's a regular imposter, and Kilbeg should rout her out of the place.'

But the people somehow did not warm to this view. The very suddenness of the woman's appearance, the mystery of her coming, and the uncertainty of her authority to occupy Nan Hogan's house, gave her an interest that was not without its magic for Kilbeg. They would not like to see her routed, and to Sara Finnessy's battle call there was no response.

But Sara Finnessy felt too strongly on the matter to remain inactive. There was a little thrill of excitement — not unmixed with delight — when she was seen stepping over the stile and walking down to Nan Hogan's house with an air of grim determination.

Maura Casey was seated in from the doorway darning a stocking, when the shadow of Sara Finnessy fell across her. Maura Casey's fingers twitched a little when she looked up.

'Come, you imposter, clear out of this place.'

Sara Finnessy's attitude was one of battle right from the start. She wrapped the little shawl across her shoulders with a movement that held a threat. She stepped into Nan Hogan's house.

Maura Casey backed away from her.

'You're Sara Finnessy?' she asked.

'Mrs. Sara Finnessy, by your leave, well known to Kilbeg, and all belonging to me likewise.'

Sara Finnessy cleared her throat in anticipation for a lengthy warfare, and she had a pleasant feeling that Maura Casey had not much of a tongue. The tongue was the only weapon known to the womenfolk of Kilbeg, and Sara Finnessy felt conscious of her strength. But Maura Casey had travelled much, and had seen many sights. She had had her mind broadened on the resources of civilisation in times of grave crisis. Her hand went out for the broom of heather that stood behind the door.

'Quit your sweeping and give me your rights to this place,' Sara Finnessy demanded imperiously.

Sara Finnessy got the first stroke of the broom on the side of the head. She staggered over to the little window, her hands to her head. Like all incompetent people who rely too much on the power of words she was completely demoralised by the first touch of well-directed action.

'Uff,' said Maura Casey, and this time Sara Finnessy had it on the poll. She made a dash for the door, and as she reached it the thud caught her between the shoulders. Sara Finnessy staggered across the threshold, and as the people who stood out on the road awaiting developments saw her face a little murmur of amazement broke out amongst them.

Sara Finnessy made a sprint for the stile, but Maura Casey was on her heels. She swung the broom as if she were a juggler with an Indian club.

'Uff!' Maura Casey grunted every time she caught her mark. When Sara Finnessy half tumbled over the stile she began to shout for Christy, but Christy was at home, making a horse of himself on the floor for the children.

Maura Casey stood on the stile with her broom, and watched Sara Finnessy running up the road home, her hair flying behind her. The people standing before Maura Casey on the road broke out into an ill-suppressed shout, not unmixed with laughter and admiration.

'Bedad,' a man said, 'that's the quickest bit of work I saw since the Boherlahan Races.'

'Who'd think Sara Finnessy could be put down in two minutes?' a woman spoke up. 'The devil's cure to her!' she cried.

'Now, me hearties,' Maura Casey declared, as she poised on the stile, looking like a parody of Galatea on the Pedestal, 'I'll do for Kilbeg what the schoolmaster never did for it. I'll teach it some manners.'

And she turned into Nan Hogan's house, feeling victorious but not happy. If the people could see her five minutes after, they would behold her lying face downward on the bed in the little room, sobbing hysterically.

Sara Finnessy was not seen for the rest of the evening. Neither was her man, Christy.

'God help Christy,' the Widow Lowry said with a queer look on her face.

When Fardy Lalor went in to Meg he sat down on a chair, and laughed until the baby threatened him with his fat kithogue.

'Praise be to God,' Fardy said 'to see that little woman putting Mrs. Finnessy over the stile. She scattered Sara's hairpins east and west.'

For the rest of the week Maura Casey devoted herself to her duties in Nan Hogan's house with unabated vigour. But the question of her occupancy was, as Paul Manton had said, a matter to be settled by the law.

The law came in the shape of Tim O'Halloran. Tim was agent for the landlord of Nan Hogan's house and the other houses in Kilbeg. They were not a valuable property. 'They brought in a few shillings,' was Tim O'Halloran's way of putting it.

Tim O'Halloran was surprised to hear that Nan Hogan's house was occupied by Maura Casey, but, like the wise man that he was, he did not express any opinion on the point to the people of Kilbeg. He looked thoughtfully down upon the road for some time and then went in to interview Maura Casey.

Kilbeg never knew what transpired at the interview, but when Tim O'Halloran came out he headed for Mrs. McDermott's farmhouse at the Lough.

'You might as well be giving her an odd day when you have it. She says she often worked in the fields and is a good warrant to weed,' Tim O'Halloran said.

'I'll give her a trial,' Mrs. McDermott said. 'But wasn't she a venturesome woman to as good as break into the house?'

'Well, she's in it now, and the house is the better of her. Not a taste she had to live on but a bag of potatoes and a grain of tea. She had a few shillings leaving the Poorhouse.'

'But what's going to happen if Nan Hogan comes out of the hospital and finds the strange woman in her house?'

Tim O'Halloran's long face broke into one of those wintry smiles that sometimes passed over it.

'That'll be a matter for another day,' he said. 'We must take some things in this world by instalments, and at the last leave a lot of reckoning to the Almighty.'

That day Maura Casey threw open her front door to the world. Kilbeg took it as a declaration of her independence. The law had given her its sanction, but the news got out that up to this Maura Casey had been, as Mrs. Finnessy surmised, 'a regular imposter'.

'Well,' Paul Manton said to his woman, 'Tim O'Halloran knows his own business best, but it's a strange turn in the history of Nan Hogan's house.'

'She looks secure enough,' Mrs. Paul Manton replied, 'but believe you me, she'll have a queer stroke of fortune in front of her when Nan Hogan comes out.'

Paul slapped his knee with his hand. 'Out she'll come,' he declared. 'It'll be one of the greatest sights ever seen in Kilbeg when Nan Hogan stands there on one side of the threshold and Maura Casey stands on the other.'

'Nan Hogan has the rights of the house,' Mrs. Manton declared. 'Every stick in the place belongs to her. It's queer law if she's bested out of her place, and I'd say that if Tim O'Halloran had the wisdom of every saint on the calendar.'

Maura Casey was given an odd day's work by the neighbouring farmers. She went up and down the village with an independent gait. Sara Finnessy called things after her a few times as she passed, but as Sara Finnessy took care to call out from the battlements of her own citadel, Maura Casey went her way if not in peace, at least in silence.

There was no word of Nan Hogan's homecoming and Maura Casey was steadily improving her position. Not a week passed that she did not effect some change in the house, for she worked with all the enthusiasm of one new to her art and careless of the conventions. She was whitewashing at a time when no person had ever seen whitewashing in Kilbeg before. Once she brought home the remains of a pot of crimson paint, and Kilbeg opened its eyes when it saw the sashes of Nan Hogan's windows flaring out at them from the white of the walls. So struck was Maura herself with the effect that next day she started to paint the door. But the paint gave out when only half the door had been covered, so that the contrast between the half that was crimson and the half that was of the drab, common to all doors in Kilbeg, proved really startling. No sooner had the sensation of the door died down than Kilbeg learned that Maura Casey had gotten a clucking hen and a setting of eggs. Two geraniums planted in tin canisters made their appearance on the window sill. Cheap coloured prints were going up on the kitchen walls with a rapidity that took away the breath of Kilbeg. When anybody was seen going down to Maura Casey some of the neighbours asked, 'Is it going down to see the picture gallery you are?' Nan Hogan's taste in house decoration had been of the most ascetic description, so that the people began to wonder what she would say, and, still more, what she would do, if she ever turned up in Kilbeg again.

'Be this and be that,' said Paul Manton, 'unless Nan Hogan gathers her legs under her soon she won't know her own house when she sees it.'

Mrs. Paul Manton felt the weight of the wrong to Nan Hogan and to her house pressing so heavily upon her mind that one day she made a journey to Boherlahan and paid a visit to Nan Hogan in the hospital.

Nan Hogan received her with much scepticism, and took the opportunity of giving vent to many fresh complaints of Kilbeg, which she had evolved in her mind in the enforced quiet of the place.

When, however, Mrs. Paul Manton cleared her throat, looked cautiously up and down the ward, leaned in over the bed, and whispered to the patient, Nan Hogan's eye became very fixed and stern, and her mouth drawn and tight.

'And there she is in your house to this hour, Nan, as cocked up with herself as if she owned Kilbeg,' Mrs. Manton concluded.

'The treachery of Kilbeg,' Nan Hogan murmured sadly at last, 'the treachery of Kilbeg.'

'Kilbeg isn't to blame,' Mrs. Manton ventured.

Nan Hogan's eye came round slowly, and fixed itself searchingly on Mrs. Manton's flushed face.

'To say,' said Nan Hogan, 'that there was a whole village full of ye there, one bigger and abler than another, and for all that a handful of a woman could defy ye all! To say that the little place of a woman stretched in her sickness was at the mercy of the first wanderer on the roads — leave me alone!'

Nan Hogan turned towards the wall with a sigh.

Mrs. Paul Manton endeavoured to comfort and coax her, but Nan Hogan kept her face to the wall. 'I don't want ever to see Kilbeg again,' she would say, 'or one belonging to it. I'm done with Kilbeg for ever.'

When Mrs. Manton got out of the hospital she wiped the perspiration from her face. 'I'd be better pleased,' she told herself, 'if I never set foot in this place. Nan Hogan is done for now.'

Nan Hogan lay in bed all night with her face to the wall. But in the morning she sat up suddenly in bed and looked about her with a changed face. There was an eagerness, an agitation, in her expression, a battle-light in her eye. Before half an hour there was witnessed in the Boherlahan Hospital a scene which upset all medical theories and confounded all scientific reasoning. The nurses were horrified to see Nan Hogan struggle out of bed and attempt to walk upon the floor. She swayed about a little in her nightdress, then held on to the head of the bed. They went to her assistance and persuaded her to lie down. But every half hour Nan Hogan was up again 'practising for a dance,' as one of the other patients put it. Neither the nuns nor the nurses could get any good of Nan Hogan. She wanted the strength of her limbs, she told them, and was going her own way about getting it. For three days Nan Hogan shocked the medical adviser and worried the nurses, but by the third day she was able to walk about.

'I'll be leaving this place now,' she announced, 'and if there is any justice in Heaven I'll never see it again. I'll fight Kilbeg from Mary Hickey's house down to my own cabin before they get me into the Poorhouse Car again.'

Pa Cloone was driving from Boherlahan and gave Nan Hogan a lift when she came out into the world once more. Nan sat on a sack of hay, taking the familiar scene in with her unsympathetic eye as she drove to Kilbeg. She spoke no word to Pa Cloone, and Pa's expression was one of extraordinary but well-suppressed delight. He left Nan down at the side leading to her cabin. They had driven quietly through the village, but already the people were rushing from their houses and surrounding Nan, shaking her hands and giving her welcome. Nan's voice rose over the turmoil.

'Quit your lies and stand back from my path,' she cried. 'Kilbeg had always treachery in its heart.'

The people hung back a little as Nan struggled over the stile. Her eye was riveted on her cabin.

'Did the world ever see such conduct,' she shouted, pointing to the door in all its half-painted glory. 'Making a mock of my house, and robbing me of all my belongings.'

The door was opened, and Maura Casey stood on the doorstep with a dishcloth in her hand. When she beheld Nan Hogan the dishcloth fell from her unnerved fingers and she stepped back. Nan came down to the door and stood before it. Maura Casey was drawn up inside, a flush of anxiety on her cheeks. The two women stared at each other for a little while, Nan Hogan's head drawn a little to one side, owing to the exigencies of her one eye.

'Can it be,' Nan asked at last, 'that you have the assurance to stand there in front of me?'

'Come into the house,' Maura Casey made answer, nervously.

Nan backed away a step.

'I'll go into my house surely,' she said, 'but not until the air of it is fit for a Christian. Out you come, Maura Casey, you whipster, and never show your face in Kilbeg again.'

Maura Casey stood her ground.

'Come into the house,' she repeated.

'Never!' Nan Hogan cried, waving her arms dramatically. 'Never, so long as you stand upon my floor. Back with you to the fit place you left behind you.'

The people craned their necks over the wall at the stile, breathlessly following the struggle. It went on for a long while. Maura Casey said little, but Nan Hogan said much. She painted an imaginary career for Maura Casey which lacked neither force nor scandal.

'Well,' Maura Casey said at last, 'if you won't come in, stay where you are.' And she closed out the door.

Nan Hogan turned her attention for some time to the people of Kilbeg, and what she had to say to them was not flattering. Mrs. Manton and the Widow Lowry made unavailing efforts to bring about an understanding between the two women. Nan Hogan would not go into the house, and Maura Casey would not come out of it. There was no getting the situation beyond this deadlock.

'As I said before,' Paul Manton declared, 'it's all a matter of the law.'

'The treachery of Kilbeg!' Nan Hogan declared, turning her eye to heaven in mute appeal.

'Tim O'Halloran has the settling of it all,' Paul Manton insisted. 'He left the house to Maura Casey, and it belongs to Nan Hogan. Let Tim O'Halloran mend what he made if he has logic enough for it.'

Nan Hogan walked over to the closed door, and putting her back to it, sat down upon the threshold, raising an ologone that went out over the hills.

The people's sympathies were all with Nan Hogan. She was one of themselves, and Maura Casey was a stranger. But the men were loth to carry out an eviction, to, as one of them said, 'make dirty bailiffs and black-livered emergencymen of ourselves'. If it happened to be a man who held the fort they would have kicked him out on the road long ago, but when it came to laying a hand on a little handful of a woman they sought excuses. If any force were considered necessary there was an impression that it was a case for the women, but the women remembered how Sara Finnessy had fared. There was a suggestion of strength and fight and determination in the closed-out door and the quiet of the house that Maura Casey held. She was sitting tight, holding on to the nine points of the law which she held within her grasp. The people were uncertain and baffled, and at once agreed with Paul Manton that it was a case for Tim O'Halloran. Accordingly, a jennet was tackled to a cart and two young fellows posted hot foot to Boherlahan to acquaint Tim O'Halloran with the extraordinary situation which he had created in Kilbeg.

'Well,' said Tim O'Halloran, when he had been acquainted with the facts, 'Boherlahan is a wide union and a wild union, with mountains and lakes and forests and many strange people, but there is more torment to be got in a corner of Kilbeg than in the length and breadth of it.'

On the way to Kilbeg Tim O'Halloran did some quiet thinking, and the gossoons who drove the cart concluded that he was trying to solve in his mind the problem concerning Nan Hogan's house.

However, when they reached Kilbeg they were astonished that Tim O'Halloran refused to be driven straight to the scene of action. Instead, he ordered them to let him down at Paul Manton's door, and he at once held a council of war in the kitchen. He sat rubbing his chin, while the people came in to give him the full details of the situation. Nan Hogan continued to sit on the door-step of the house, caoining and lamenting and going over the troubles of her life, while Maura Casey lay low within.

'Where is Sara Finnessy?' Tim O'Halloran asked at last.

'Above in her own house. She's afraid to show her nose on account of the skelping she got.'

'Send her down to me,' Tim O'Halloran ordered.

It took a big deputation and a great deal of persuasion to induce Sara Finnessy to make her appearance, but at last she came.

Tim O'Halloran ordered the people out of the kitchen, and was left alone with Sara Finnessy.

'This is a bad business,' Tim began.

'It's a business that has no concern for me at all, Tim O'Halloran,' Sara made answer.

'I think you're mistaken in that, Sara.'

'Devil a bit, then.'

'You and Nan Hogan have been a long time at daggers drawn.'

'If we have, that's Nan Hogan's fault.'

'I know it is, Sara. But this business of the house is all in your hands now. You're the one person in the world to settle it.'

'Me?' Sara Finnessy exclaimed, looking at Tim O'Halloran incredulously.

'No other, Sara.'

Sara laughed sarcastically.

'It's your one chance in the world to make it up with Nan Hogan.'

'There's no making up with the like of her.'

'It's for you to go down and rout Maura Casey out of the house in front of Nan. That'll make up the breach.

'Is it to face Maura Casey? And she like a badger below in the house.'

'She'll be too much afeard to fight this time, Sara.'

'I wouldn't face her for the weight of Kilbeg in gold — except I had a hatchet or something,' Sara added, grimly.

'Look here, Sara Finnessy,' Tim O'Halloran said, rousing himself, 'there's nothing thought of you by the people since Maura Casey put you out over the stile. You have no respect in Kilbeg since that, and if you be wishful to remove that stain and make it up with Nan Hogan now's your chance. And if you do it well there won't be one thought half as much of as yourself for the rest of your life. It's a great chance entirely for you, Sara Finnessy.'

'I tell you it would take a hatchet, Tim O'Halloran,' Sara Finnessy insisted, but Tim, with some satisfaction, saw a look of ambition beginning to show in the face of Sara Finnessy.

'Go in by the back door, grab the broom, and drive her out with it over the stile before the eyes of Nan Hogan and of Kilbeg. Where you made the blunder before was not to grab the broom first. It was all a matter of who had it first.'

'She might rise the tongs to me,' Sara suggested.

'Don't give her time. But she won't. She's too much in dread of the people now. They'll be around the house. I'll have a few gossoons ready to go in if she takes the tongs at you.'

Tim pressed home the case, and Sara Finnessy came round gradually. By the time she stepped out of the house, her inherent love of conflict was burning in her eyes. She wanted to pay off Maura Casey for the crushing humiliation she had put upon her. Her fingers were twitching for the broom as she set forth to the battle.

Tim O'Halloran raised a coal on the tongs to light his pipe, and then settled himself comfortably in his chair, that fleeting, wintry smile passing over his long face.

Sara Finnessy acted on Tim O'Halloran's plan of campaign. She got quietly to the back of Nan Hogan's house and pushed in the door softly, then made a grab at the broom. She glanced about the kitchen. It was empty. She took a little run for the front door and threw it open.

Nan Hogan was on the top note of one of her lamentations when she felt the door at her back swing open. She glanced round, gathered herself to her feet, and panted at the sight of the apparition before her. Sara Finnessy swung the broom over her head, her eyes wild-looking and excited.

At the same moment Maura Casey stepped out from the little room. She took in the situation with a glance and stood perfectly still, her back to the wall.

'God leave me my reason,' Nan Hogan exclaimed, 'but is it Sara Finnessy I see in my house?'

'Out of the woman's house,' Maura Casey exclaimed.

Sara Finnessy made a wild sweep of the broom at Maura Casey. It swept Maura's face, and the next instant Maura had one end of it in her hands. Sara thought to jerk it from her, but Maura Casey was accustomed to hold on to whatever little things came within her grasp in life.

There was a little scuffle over by the room door. Sara Finnessy often declared afterwards that she would have won the day only the sight became scattered in her eyes. As it was, she felt Maura Casey pressing her against the wall, and the next thing that she remembered was to feel hard, long fingers about the scruff of her neck. A quiver went down her spine, for she knew at once that they were the bony fingers of Nan Hogan. She got a few jerks from behind, and felt herself staggering over the threshold of the door. She was conscious of a jeering murmur in a crowd of onlookers outside, and with a last desperate effort turned back to the door, her hands out for the first enemy that came within her reach.

'Close out the door or she'll murder us!' Nan Hogan cried, and the door was slapped out on Sara Finnessy's face. She beat her hands on the door in vain. But as the crowd was becoming greater and more boisterous at the stile, and as the door was secured inside, Sara Finnessy was much relieved to feel Christy's hand on her shoulder.

'Come home out of this,' Christy said.

'I will,' Sara cried hysterically. 'I'll leave them to the judgment of God.'

When Tim O'Halloran, from his comfortable chair by Paul Manton's fire, saw Christy Finnessy leading his woman up home, 'and she having all the signs and tokens of ignominious defeat written upon her face,' he hitched back the chair a bit. 'It was quicker than I expected,' he said.

A moment later Mrs. Manton came running into the house.

'Was it you sent Sara Finnessy down to rout Maura Casey out of the house?' she asked.

'Aye, it was then,' Tim admitted quietly.

'Well, you only made bad worse,' Mrs. Manton said.

'And are the other two inside now?' Tim asked.

'They are, and the sorra a word or sign out of them.'

'Very well,' Tim said. 'I'll be on my way home now. This business has nearly cost me the length of a day, and I having many a thing to attend to.'

Mrs. Manton looked after Tim O'Halloran as he struck

up the Boherlahan road, a puzzled look on her face. Gradually a light broke in upon her, and her face lengthened out. She sat down on a chair, folded her arms, and wagged her head slowly. 'Well,' she said at last, 'the devil is shook on you, Tim O'Halloran.'

However, things were not so quiet inside Nan Hogan's house as the people thought. Nan was rather excited, for Sara Finnessy's thumps on the door frightened her while they lasted. Maura Casey, on the other hand, stood drawn to one side of the door, the broom gripped ready in her hand. It was just as well for Sara Finnessy that the door held out. When Christy was heard leading his woman away, Maura Casey left the broom carefully behind the door. Nan Hogan sank into a chair with a sigh.

'Well,' said Nan at last. 'I came in, after all, Maura Casey. You may thank Sara Finnessy for it, or a step I'd never take on the floor while you were here.'

'When did you leave the hospital?' Maura asked, mildly.

'This morning, thank God,' Nan replied. 'And I was no sooner seen by the stile outside than the cut-throats of Kilbeg came running down to welcome me. When I get my strength back I'll let them know what I have weighing on my mind.'

Maura Casey fixed up the fire on the hearth and set the kettle to boil. Nan's eye followed her movements with growing scorn. When Maura Casey reached out for the teapot on the dresser Nan turned on her.

'Don't lay a hand on that teapot,' she cried. 'Don't think you're going to come round me. I'm not as soft as you fancy, Maura Casey.'

Maura laid down the teapot and turned to Nan. Her face was troubled and anxious-looking.

'Won't you let me be in the house with you?' she asked.

'Is it my house to hold the scruff of Boherlahan?' Nan demanded.

'I'm used to the house now. I wouldn't like the thoughts of the roads again.'

'It's little concern I have for your thoughts.'

'I could be doing many a thing for you. I could be working at the farmers' places an odd day and bringing in a few shillings.'

'You can work when and where you wish, but you'll be cutting your stick out of this place.'

'You're not too well yet, Nan Hogan. If you get taken with the weakness again they'll be bringing you back into hospital.'

'No,' Nan cried, with some alarm. 'The Poorhouse Car will never stand at my door again.'

'Tim O'Halloran will find means of getting you out.'

Nan Hogan looked out the window with her one eye, her mouth twitching a little. Maura Casey could see the shadow of a great terror falling across her face.

'Don't be upsetting me with your talk,' Nan said at last. 'You can make a shake down for yourself in the corner here for tonight. It's too late for the roads now. But tomorrow morning you'll gather together whatever things you have belonging to you in this place and leave my house.'

Nan walked into the room and closed out the door. Maura Casey heard her shooting the bolt on the inside. She sat down by the fire miserably. After all, it was a hard thing to face the wandering life again when she had tasted the sweets of a home. Now and then Maura Casey's eyes would travel about the kitchen, lingering on articles which had become dear to her. She stayed by the fire the best part of the night, crying quietly to herself. Then she made a sort of bed by the hearth and slept a little.

In the morning Maura Casey renewed the fire. She scattered some crumbs on the floor for the hen and her young brood, and did other duties about the place. Then she heard Nan Hogan shooting the bolt from the door.

'Maura Casey,' Nan called.

Maura Casey pushed in the room door. Nan Hogan was sitting up in bed, having only reached out to draw the bolt.

'What noise is that I heard? Is it a stray hen that came in

with a clutch of chickens?'

'She's my own hen. I got her and the eggs from Mrs. O'Hea. Eleven of them she brought out. A body wouldn't feel until the like of them would be laying fine eggs.'

'Well,' Nan said, 'you can be bringing them with you.'

'I'll leave them where they are. What way could I contrive to bring them, Nan Hogan?'

'As to that flower pot,' Nan said, pointing to the geranium in the canister on the window, 'It's not wholesome. You can be giving it to one of the children.'

'Are you getting up now, Nan Hogan?' Maura Casey asked, measuring Nan Hogan's attitude in the bed with a shrewdness that was bringing a ray of hope into her heart.

'Not now,' Nan said, a little disconcerted.

'Aren't you feeling well?' Maura insisted, stepping in a little way to the room.

Nan Hogan's eye fell.

'I'm feeling elegant,' she said.

'You haven't the weakness in the legs again?'

'I over-reached myself yesterday. I'll be all right by and by.'

Maura Casey went out into the kitchen and returned after some time with a cup of tea and some toast. Without a word she laid them in Nan Hogan's lap as she sat on the bed, and walked out again.

Presently the rain came down in torrents. Maura Casey stood at the door looking out over the wet country. 'It would be a hard day on the roads,' she said to herself.

When she went into the room again the tea and the toast had disappeared. Nan Hogan was still sitting up in bed, a great brown beads in her hands, swaying a little from side to side, as she recited the Rosary.

Maura Casey took up the cup and saucer and turned to leave the room. Nan Hogan paused in her devotions and looked at Maura Casey.

'What time will you be quitting this place?' she asked.

'The rain is very heavy,' Maura Casey made answer.

'Tell me, Maura Casey,' Nan went on, 'had you ever anyone belonging to you sailing the waters of the oceans?'

'Never,' Maura answered, 'I was always alone.'

'I have a son on the seas,' Nan said, 'and the rest of my care are in heaven. I do be praying to them to send him back to me.'

And Nan Hogan went on with her prayers.

Maura Casey went out into the kitchen. She made spasmodic efforts to do a few things about the place. But she spent most of the time listening with alert ears for any sound of stirring in the room, her hands twitching, opening and clasping as she listened. Every now and then she would murmur under her breath, 'She might never be able to put them under her again.'

The day was drawing to a close when the room door opened, and Nan Hogan came out dressed and walking a little helplessly.

'Did any of the traitors of Kilbeg ask to darken my door today?' she asked, coming out.

'An odd one of them was crossing the stile,' Maura Casey said, 'but I said it was not your wish for any of them to come in. I told them you were in a long sleep after the fatigue of your sickness.'

Nan Hogan gave a little grunt of satisfaction. 'They might be in no hurry to face me,' she said, 'when I gather the clearness of my mind together.'

Maura Casey moved to the door and looked up at the sky. 'The rain is coming heavy yet,' she said.

Nan Hogan went down and sat by the fire.

'Well,' she said, 'I ought to be thankful to the mercy of God that I am by my own fire again. Another month of that rotten place in Boherlahan and the heart would be broke across in me.'

'The comfort of a house is a great thing surely,' Maura Casey said, standing at the door, looking out over the desolate country, her eyes following the mist that rose and broke upon the hills.

Nan Hogan looked at Maura Casey with her sharp eye. 'You look very drooping in yourself,' she said. 'You're like an old sick hen that'd stay up on the perch the hours of the day, the wings hanging by her.'

'I'm thinking of the deep roads and the pair of boots I have,' Maura Casey said.

'Aye,' Nan Hogan went on, raising the tongs to settle up the fire, 'there do be many a turn and twist in the story that stretches behind a person's life. I suppose a day or two ago you were standing out there in the sun, pluming your fine feathers, and thinking all to yourself that Nan Hogan would never gather a leg under her to go between you and the grabbing of her house.'

'There was no grabbing about it,' Maura Casey answered. 'I kept it well with the activity of my two hands, Nan Hogan.'

Maura Casey came in from the door, and took down a thin shawl from a nail on the backdoor, which she threw over her shoulders. 'The rain is over now,' she said.

Nan Hogan stood up and went to the door, halting and limping. She looked up at the sky.

'You could be putting no more trust in that sky,' she said, 'than you could be depending on the neighbourly grace of Kilbeg.'

'I'll be on my road now, Nan Hogan,' Maura Casey answered.

Nan did not pretend to hear her as she stood at the door. 'Look at the big, loaded cloud up from the West. It'll be washing every blade of grass on the hills.'

She closed out the door and limped back to the fire. Then her eyes ranged over the flaring pictures on the walls, the faces of patriots and politicians, saints and writers, staring from a hoarding of caricatures. 'Please God,' Nan said, ranging her disapproving eye over them, 'I'll make a bonfire of them tomorrow.'

Maura Casey paused a little, looking intently at Nan Hogan. Nan sat down in her old seat by the fire, then reached out for a stool which she settled the other side of the hearth.

'Maura Casey,' Nan said, 'I was speaking to you today about that son of mine travelling the wide waters of the world. He was taken from under this roof by the greatest rascal that ever left the heart of a woman stripped of its comfort. Sit down here until I be telling you of the grace and beauty of the boy that went sailoring from me.'

Maura Casey's fingers trembled a little as she hung the shawl up on the nail. She went over and sat down on the stool by Nan Hogan's hearth.

When the night had fallen on Kilbeg, two carefully shawled figures, with enough space in front of the faces to allow a single eye to see out, stole very noiselessly over the stile leading down to Nan Hogan's house and crept cautiously up to the little window, through which they peered into the kitchen. Outlined against the fire they could see two distinct figures sitting on two stools — the figure of Nan Hogan and the figure of Maura Casey. Nan Hogan was speaking, leaning a hand on Maura Casey's arm as she spoke. Maura Casey was listening very intently, every now and then turning her head away from Nan and wiping something from her eyes surreptitiously.

The Widow Lowry's elbow nudged Mrs. Paul Manton at the window outside. The Widow's shawled head stooped over to Mrs. Manton's shawled head.

'She's telling her the troubles of her life,' the Widow whispered. 'Little wonder she's drawing tears from her.'

Mrs. Manton's head nodded in agreement. 'They look like a pair of well-matched cronies,' she whispered back. 'It'll be the making of Nan Hogan to have someone to discourse to by the fire in the night.'

'And if she ever gets taken sick again she'll have one at hand accustomed to handle cases like hers.'

'It's my opinion,' the Widow Lowry said, 'that Tim O'Halloran was working for this end all the while.'

'He's a caution when it comes to a matter of clever

stratagems. He has the understanding of the world. See how he used Sara Finnessy to bring them two creatures together.'

'Look! They are going upon their knees by the hearth. Nan is taking out her Rosary Beads.'

The Man with the Gift

For twenty-five years the Boss had gone up and down the worn cabin steps without a worry. His fists had grown accustomed to the feel of ropes, to the rolling up and down of barrels, and the swinging of boxes, at the loading and discharging of *The Golden Barque*. The motion of his limbs had come to be part of the ritual of the deck. He exhaled an odour of tar. His feet had flattened, his hands had rounded, his neck had developed a curve, throwing his face forward. His eyes were palely yellow, like the water of the canal. His vision had become concentrated, drilling through the landscape like canals. His temperament was placid. His emotions rose and fell as mechanically as if they were regulated by invisible locks. He was as tame as a duck. His name was Martin Coughlan, and he was known, by stray words that followed his speech like a memory, to have come from the North.

The torch of democracy — organisation — one day reached the backwash of existence. It found by its strange devices, of all people, Martin Coughlan. Up to that he had no sense of responsibility for the wrongs of the world, no brooding of the spirit in the problems of his day. His interests began at one harbour and ended at another. The things that he saw from the deck made up his world. They were good, and he was satisfied.

But then they came to him and told him he had been elected on the Committee. He beamed at the announcement, for he grasped, though vaguely, that he was a man chosen, one to whom honour was paying her respects. He walked into the shed where they held the Committee meetings with his slow lurch, his mind a blank as to the purpose of the assembly. He made no inquiries. He sat down with the others and looked around him. A man at a table read something out of a book. Martin Coughlan laughed, and felt the others staring at him.

A deep voice, with a note of admonition, if not tragedy, called out 'Order'. Martin Coughlan poked the ribs of a neighbour to show that he appreciated the humour of the situation.

Then a man rose at the head of the table. He was a spare man with drooping moustachios, a penetrating eye, a voice that sounded high and sharp in the shed.

Martin Coughlan stared at the speaker. Something rare and unsuspected had touched his life. He wondered where this spare man had got all the words. They came out in a steady flow. He was obviously aiming at something, but what it was Martin Coughlan did not know and, indeed, did not care. It was sufficient for him that the words came on and on. He had never heard any mortal before keeping up such a sustained flood of speech. Martin Coughlan leaned back, delight on his face.

Another man rose. He spoke, even better. He gesticulated with energy. The others began to slap their limbs with their hands. Martin Coughlan slapped his limbs, feeling he was privileged. He had begun to live.

A thick-set man followed. His voice wakened echoes all over the place. His eyes flashed around, seeking one face now, another again. Suddenly the eyes fell on Martin Coughlan; the man addressed him as if he were appealing to an intelligence! He argued with him, made gestures at him, deposited all his logic at his feet.

Martin Coughlan's blood began to heat. He felt a tingle at the curve on the back of his neck. He coughed to relieve the tension. Then the speaker's gaze wandered to somebody else.

The talk went on for some hours. Men grew excited. Several spoke at the same time for pregnant minutes. Martin Coughlan began to perspire. Once he shouted, 'Hear, hear', because the words had begun to sound familiar.

When the Committee meeting broke up he went back to the boat, his cheeks flaming, feeling that he had done it all himself. He passed Hike on the way. The little driver looked up at him with respect. The dark-faced man was sitting on a box by the stern.

'The meeting over?' he asked.

'Yes,' Martin Coughlan said.

His voice sounded hoarse. His throat felt dry. He went down to the keg and drank a mug of water.

Afterwards Martin Coughlan paced the deck with a new air. He became preoccupied. Once they saw him gesticulating at a bush on the bank. He took a new tone to the lock-keepers. He was always clearing his throat.

A few times at the meals they thought he was about to make a speech. But something always overcame him. When they sounded him as to the Committee proceedings his face beamed.

'There was speech-making,' he would say.

'What did they say?'

Martin Coughlan rose. He caught the lapel of his coat; struck an attitude. An inspired look came into his face. But no words followed. Instead he took up a bucket and went on deck.

'He's a great man for the Committee,' they said. 'He won't give the show away.'

'Aye, man, but that fellow is knowing. He could hold a Cabinet secret.'

One day the dark-faced man loaned a paper at a village.

'They don't give the speeches,' he said, 'but there is the name right enough — Martin Coughlan.'

Martin Coughlan took the paper. His eyes swam as he spelled out his name. He pored over the sheet for long spells throughout the rest of the evening. When the men were turning in he said: 'Boys, but she's a brave wee paper.'

He got a candle, and sat over it, spelling everything out, including the advertisements. Then he sat up, delight on his face, the look in his eyes of a man who knew he had achieved something. 'Men,' he said, 'I've overhauled her, beam and aft, stem to stern.'

But the only answer was a chorus of heavy snores. He turned in with a grumble.

There was another Committee meeting soon after. The speeches fell on his head like dew from the heavens. Language! Why, the world had never yet heard the like. Moreover, he became conscious that the other men were deferring to him in their views. He sat there as solemn as a judge, the greatest listener who had ever arrived in the shed. The speakers felt that they had at last got hold of an audience, a man of appreciation. Now and then he nodded his head in approval. It was worth a yard of debate. When he shook his head in disapproval it excited the speakers. They went on and on, fighting, arguing, playing for his opinion. But Martin Coughlan held to his silent views with wonderful pugnacity. He was not to be cajoled.

'What were they at last night, Martin?' one of the men asked afterwards.

'That,' said Martin, after a pause, 'is a secret.'

'He's too close-minded,' they said. 'He keeps it all in for the Committee. It must be something to hear him when the cork is off.'

The dark-faced man was fond of his paper. He got it regularly in the village. 'Here we are,' he said, with satisfaction. 'They give us the speeches this time. Now we'll know what Martin Coughlan had to say for himself.'

But there was no speech from Martin Coughlan. Everybody had said something except the representative from *The Golden Barque*.

The dark-faced man made a complaint.

'Don't mind the paper,' Martin Coughlan said. 'She is no good. I knew from the first she had sprung a leak.'

But he felt that the men were dissatisfied. He struck an attitude on the deck, and said: 'Mr. Chairman and gentlemen — I venture to think.' He paused. 'To my mind,' he added. There was another pause. 'I say, standing here tonight.' He looked vaguely over the landscape. 'I beg to propose.' And then he took a little run up and down the deck, rubbing his hands with delight.

'He's too clever,' one of the men said. 'He thinks to put us off by play-acting. It won't do.'

Before the proceedings of the next Committee meeting began, Martin Coughlan took the secretary aside. The secretary was a shrewd person. There was a motion on the agenda to give him a salary.

'John,' said Martin Coughlan, with familiarity, 'I want you to tell me how it is done.'

'How is what done?'

'The speeches, you know; the language, the words, the talk they do have.'

John was puzzled. Then a light broke upon him.

'Well,' he said, 'a man must have it in him.'

'Have what in him?'

John hesitated, thought, and said. 'The gift.'

Martin Coughlan was crestfallen. He felt there was something in life he had let slip.

'Where would there be likelihood of getting the gift?' he asked at last.

'I don't know,' the other replied. 'It comes from within.'

'Oh, I see,' Martin Coughlan said, more cheerfully. Then he confided, 'John, I have it within in the inside of me. Language, great language. But I can't get it out.'

'Have courage,' the other said. 'Take your chance. Get up on your legs. Face them. When you do that the words will flow out of you.'

'Do you think they will, John?'

'Sure.' John was a man persuasive, one who carried conviction, inspired hope — and drew salaries.

'Then there is that wee paper, John. If I'd come out with

the words, they would be there, of course. They do be reading her, looking out for what a man might say.'

'Oh, that's it, is it, Martin?' John asked, then patted the other on the back. 'That will be all right, old man. Leave that to me. Vote straight on the salary question, and the goods will be delivered to you on the paper.'

'Thanks, John; I will.'

At a critical moment in the debate, Martin Coughlan rose. He went over to the table, rapped his knuckles upon it to command attention, jerked the collar of his coat about his neck. He struck the attitude he had rehearsed aboard. It was reminiscent of various statues erected to the memory of great orators.

He looked up and down the shed. A hush fell upon the assembly. Men leaned back to hear what the silent man, the audience, the one man of reticence among them, had to say at this crisis.

'Mr. Chairman and Mr. Gentlemen.' Martin Coughlan began, blundering through nervousness.

There was a laugh. Martin Coughlan moistened his lips with his tongue, for they were dry and inclined to stick. One of his knees struck against the other. Then he had to clear a lump from his throat.

'John, our secretary,' he said at last, 'told me that if I stood up on me legs the words would flow out from within the inside of me.'

He hesitated, looking about him in a panic, a queer feeling of collapse in his brain. He smiled a ghastly smile.

'Go on,' said the chairman.

'He said,' Martin Coughlan resumed, his voice falling to an echo, 'that if I faced you they would flow out of me. But — by heavens — they won't.' He sat down. There was a burst of laughter and applause.

The men stared at Martin Coughlan. There was that mixture of scepticism, enjoyment, malicious delight, in their glances that fasten upon all fallen gods. They were taking their fun out of an exposure, the showing up of an emptiness that wore a mask, the betrayal of that discretion which is only a dullness.

Martin Coughlan was too heated, too full of confusion, to notice their crude levity. By the time he had recovered himself they had dropped him. They no longer deferred to him. He was no longer appealed to as an intelligence. He drew back instinctively to the shadows, and he sat there until the meeting broke up.

When he reached his boat the men greeted him with deference. He muttered something and went down to the cabin. He stayed there for the rest of the night.

'The Committee,' he said to the dark-faced man next day, 'is a rotten Committee.'

'I thought that all along,' the other replied. 'But I didn't like to say it, seeing you were a great one on it.'

'And an ignorant Committee,' Martin Coughlan added.

'It is that.'

But by the end of the week the paper was out. The dark-faced man, after reading it, looked up at Martin Coughlan and then went up to him.

'Look here, Boss,' he said, putting out his hand, 'shake hands.'

They shook hands, Martin Coughlan nervously.

'It was a great speech,' the dark-faced man said. 'You're wasting your time on this boat.'

Martin Coughlan blushed; his gaze was uncertain. The other left him the paper.

He sat on a barrel and opened the sheet. There was his name in print again! He spelled it out slowly. 'Mr. Martin Coughlan, who was received with loud applause, and —' and there followed over a column of type, of words, of language, of a speech. He read it over with a thumping heart. It was dotted with 'hear, hear', 'applause', and 'cheers'. When he finished he stood up and walked the deck, his thick limbs outspread, his flat feet solid on the planks, his chest out.

'Is it a good report, Boss?' they asked.

'It is very fair, very fair, men,' he said, with toleration.

'Man, but I'd like to hear it coming out.'

'No doubt you would.'

'We'll hear you some time.'

'You will, why not, to be sure.'

He ran his fingers through his hair. He drilled spaces, vague spaces, through the familiar landscape with his gaze. His blood rose gradually, eventually flooding his face until it grew purple in colour, rising as steadily as if somebody had lifted the sluice of a flood-gate.

'God, the language of it,' he repeated to himself over and over again throughout the day.

For the first time in his life, he refused to go into *The Haven* when they had made the journey across the bog. Instead he went into the cabin, and alone spelt the speech over and over again.

Gradually his mind got over the habit of thinking of it as something apart, something outside his own life. He no longer said, 'God, the language of it.' Instead he muttered, 'Great language; splendid talk; just the thing. That's it. That's what I'd say. That's the very word I'd say. I declare I think it was the word I said. It was going through my head at the time. I must have said that very word. If I did not, I intended it. But I forget what I said. Maybe I said it. To be sure I said it. Of course I said it. Why not? The very word; no, but the very words. If I said one word I must have said another. I could not help following up one word with another. What was to stop me? Nothing. I went on that very way. One word borrowed another. What else could it do. To be sure I said it. In fact, it's all what I said, word for word.'

He went on persuading himself until the others came back from *The Haven*.

He went up to the dark-faced man.

'I tell you what it is, it's a very fine report; a very good report; a tip-top report. Word for word there it is, in black and in white.' He struck one fist in the other.

'Boss,' the other said, something almost approaching reverence in his long, narrow face, 'you're a great one, a gifted one. For to turn round and say the like of what you said, a man must have the gift.'

'To be sure he must,' Martin Coughlan agreed taking some steps along by the cargo covered with great oil-cloths. 'I told John, the secretary, I had it within in the inside of me. And what had I within in the inside of me, I ask you, men? The gift!'

'Well, thank God we'll all hear you soon,' the dark-faced man said. 'There's a public meeting coming on.'

Martin Coughlan drew a long breath. 'You don't tell me so?'

'I do. We had word of it in *The Haven.* There is to be speech-making, and great speech-making. We'll expect you that day to show the great gift that's in you.'

'You will, to be sure,' Martin Coughlan said, but without enthusiasm. He ran his fingers through his hair. Then he walked away from the others, standing at the prow of the boat, his sturdy figure solid against the water.

'A great one he is for the gab,' the grotesque-looking man said irreverently. 'Look at the two powerful limbs he has holding him up from the ground.'

After that Martin Coughlan grew very subdued, silent, avoiding the topic of the coming meeting. The men said he was bottling himself up for the big occasion. They noted that he still pored over the paper that contained his speech. He would lie back in his bunk at night, a candle fixed by his side, drilling through the speech. Once or twice the men heard him muttering to himself like a boy grappling with a lesson. In these days it was noted that some of the colour left his face. A certain pensiveness crept into his expression.

'Boss,' one of the men asked him, 'are you in pain?'

'I am,' Martin Coughlan answered, and walked sadly away.

Once the men wakened to hear him pacing the deck in the middle of the night. The dark-faced man went up the ladder and popped his vignette over the hold. He came back after a time.

'He's on deck in his shirt,' he said. 'The moon is shining on him, his legs are like two white pillars under the tiller. He has that paper with him. I heard him giving out a few words. He was losing them, trying to catch them up again, stumbling and staggering over them like a man that would be raving. Then he would run his hands through his hair, and the wind blowing the shirt about the white pillars.'

'Be the powers,' said the grotesque man, turning over in his bunk, 'it's a chilly sort of a night, and I'm glad I have not the gift.'

As the day of the meeting approached, and it became more and more a topic of conversation, Martin Coughlan's depression increased. Something seemed to weigh him down. He took the dark-faced man aside.

'You know this meeting is got up by the Committee?' he said.

'I do.'

'And you can call to mind what I told you of that Committee a long while ago. I said it was a rotten Committee.'

'You did. I remember that.'

'And I said it was an ignorant Committee.'

'You did, right enough.'

'You agreed with me. We were at one as regards this Committee. Very well, I'm not going to give that Committee the satisfaction of making a speech for them.'

'Now, that would be a pity and you having the gift.'

'There you are! That's what makes me do it. How can a man of gift speak for a rotten, ignorant Committee?'

To the dark-faced man this was a poser. Perhaps in that moment of expediency, of pressure, Martin Coughlan showed that he had, after all, some talent for politics.

He walked down the deck with a stride.

'Never!' he exclaimed with decision, waving his arms.

The meeting came off without Martin Coughlan. He did

not even attend. He 'sent word' to strike his name off the Committee.

'We will indeed,' one of the men said. 'Little good any such tame ducks is to anyone.'

The men from *The Golden Barque* were disappointed that Martin Coughlan did not pour forth his eloquence at the assembly. They somehow regarded him as in some way wronged. But he became more cheerful himself. He began to whistle again as he moved around the boat. His flat feet became more than ever a part of the ritual of the deck. The curve at the back of his neck threw out his head another degree. His eyes became more palely yellow. They went on digging imaginary canals in the landscape. He was as happy as a duck in the water. Once the dark-faced man asked: 'Boss, what became of the paper with your speech in it?'

'Oh, yon rag!' Martin Coughlan made answer. 'I rolled her up in a stone, and she's at the bottom a wheen of weeks.'